The New Croton Review is published quarterly by the Croton Council on the Arts, Inc., a tax-exempt non-profit organization under 26 USC § 501(c)(3) in Croton-on-Hudson, New York. The editor in Chief is Jeanne-Noel Mahoney. Free (digital) subscriptions are available on the Review's website

Review.CrotonArts.org

If you'd like to submit a poem, fiction or nonfiction narrative, photograph, or a digital image of your artwork, please go to the Review's website (see above) for full details.

For other matters, you can send email to the Council at crotonarts@gmail.com, or USPS mail to CCoA, P.O.Box 277, Croton-on-Hudson NY 10520.

The original *Croton Review* was first published in the 1980's by Ruth Schechter, then president of the Croton Council on the Arts. After Ruth's tenure the Review stopped publishing for many years, and has resumed (as the *New Croton Review*) in the summer of 2022 by Jeanne-Noel Mahoney, Editor-in-Chief. Jeanne holds a PhD in English and a law degree. As director of the Black Mountain College II (SUNY Buffalo, NY), she organized the publication of the *Black Mountain II Review* which was widely distributed (even carried by City Lights, Lawrence Ferlinghetti's book store in San Francisco). In 1995 she became Executive Director of the Western New York Regional office of the New York Civil Liberties Union (a branch of the ACLU). Jeanne-Noel now lives in Croton, and is on the board of the Croton Council on the Arts.

Editor-in-Chief ……………………….. Jeanne-Noel Mahoney
Assistant Editor ……………………… Jim Christensen
Literary Editors ……………………… Stephen M. Jacoby and William Mahoney
Consultant ………………………… Valerie Leis

John C. Hart Memorial Library
1130 East Main Street

Cover and unattributed sketches in this issue by Stephen M. Jacoby, Steve@astrokid.com

Table of Contents

Hurricane Ruins
by Robert Milby

Battle worthy, universal, in a sea of sorrow, I dare!
I dare walk the tatty beach of their ruined world;
shores and shoals; fogs and folds.
I dare wander beached days where modernity died,
combing the riverside wreckage for family history —
scattered debris; shattered, melancholy, certainly *of this world,*
and destined to be in it.

Urchins now yaw in floating shacks; tents in the flooded suburbs;
flats in the darkened cities;
a stew of salvaged books, shoes and shirts —
the lottery of perpetual looting. Comfort measures for a Palm Tree,
whose trembling beauty lies dressed in capes of mud.

Each car's contents purged in a warm, tidal vomit:
pens, napkins, coffee cups and plastic bottles,
bank statements, dead cigarettes.
Restive Crows; crowds of Gulls, packing gullets in gluttony of jubilant windfall.

She can gale down a wall; bend Stop signs to submission!
He can sling trash against cars; rip flags from poles.
Why do they dash birds into trucks and buses; topple trees;
waste monuments to technology?
Why do they drown children?

God of the hot storm; a tempest with chaos, and theft in store!
Ruined lives; evil weather's water weapons —
nothing left dry, save the sailing birds, above a world upended; shattered glass; the grinding
wind worry; darkness trawling a former street; collapse of a pier; a house — demolished, as
Death calls in the debt.
The wreck and rot; parted clouds reveal the burial plot, once a shoreline paradise.

Etty's Song
by Karine Ancellin

"I shall wield this slender fountain pen as if it were a hammer and my words will have to be so many hammer strokes with which to beat the story of our fate."

I hear you Etty, your clear sounding voice
long after the ecstatic time when I first read you,
your integrity magnifies my mundane
your words lull me no leeway left,

innocent cadavers of all ages, you understand death,
all around you, made to lie in lice, amidst murky mire

and yet you don't despair, your tears call God
like Job you love and lose more, yet you hope more
so firmly, and firmer yet, How Etty, How?
Is it Spiel, or Dostoevsky feeding your resolve?

Buddha of the Shoah, my guru, my dispenser of light
I was orphaned reaching the end of your diary.

You, Etty, voice of indestructible ethics,
You dared to WRITE to the end, even on that train
you raised above all,
the other face of Nelson Mandela,
"enmeshed in century old traditions;
we still have to be born as human beings"

Today my yearning celebrates you, for your tenderness towering
over the darkest crevices of our mind.

Etty, I will sing your thoughts to the end,
as you left for Auschwitz, singing.

Picture of My Mother Over a Winter Holiday
by Jeffrey Alfier

She slumbers on the family room couch,
        wakens for a few spells to catch the MASH reruns,

then drifts again to a wider sleep. Sleet blusters
        the sliding glass door behind her

before retreating
        into the hazy silence of the gray sky.

Early evenings are the most demanding for her.
        They seem to stretch beyond the clock's patience,

my father somewhere beyond her voice —
        outside in his coal shed, or swearing

at some defiant gadget in the garage.
        In the backyard, his chestnut trees

thrum to the slow dance of the wind.
        He stays outside, scraping ice from the kitchen window.

Three Haiku
by Phyllis Kirigin

Frolic, ye mayflies
Like there is no tomorrow
Because . . . there isn't.

You're sure, little bird
You're ready to leave the
nest?
You can't go home again.

Dandelion gold
But that there are so many
You would be treasured.

Croton Point Park, photo by Andrew Courtney

Croton Landing, photo by Andrew Courtney

Mendelian Inheritance
by Susanna Case

The evening we went to hang at Dee's,
we found everyone yelling,
Dee having just discovered her father

wasn't her biological father—and therefore
her sister was only her half-sister.
Biology class had been about Gregor Mendel

and peas, and she figured it out,
though both parents had known all along,
and neither one of them had ever heard

of Mendel. Picture him puttering
in his garden in Moravia,
creating a whole new science out of seven

characteristics of peas—colors of seeds, pods,
and flowers, shape, and size—
despite having failed his exams.

Other scientists ignored Mendel—thought him
a working-class bore—the way Dee's parents
probably wished she'd ignored him

in class that day, the rupture
in her family everlasting. I couldn't fathom
giving up a perfectly good father.

Was it the genes or the years spent with the lie?
Dee's mother had lived a rough life
during wartime. The husband was a kind man

and funny—joked a lot with Dee's friends—
unlike Mendel, struggling with depression,
as later, so did Dee, a scientist now too,

as if her lineage came straight from Mendel,
who was a monk and never had any kids.
So strange, that salty stream we carry in our veins.

Invasive Species, a Love Story
by Susanna Case

A woman mistakes a bath bomb
for soap and turns a shade of pink
she can't scrub off for days, declares
she loves the product anyway.
Pink like water horses—hippos—
who turn pink in the sun from oily fluid
secreted by their glands.
Moisturizer for dry hippo skin.

I've been slathering oils on myself
this winter—orangey rosemary—to avoid
feeling hippo-like when you touch me.
One's lover shouldn't be too dry.
A folkloric painted ceramic hippo
perches atop our television cabinet.
Head bent, its eyes seem to follow us.
We joke it's FBI, with an embedded
listening device, zeroing in on two ex-hippies.
A bad pun, but anything seems possible
in this year turned inside out.

Why *not* a pink-mouthed hippo-spy—

Hippos are bad-tempered.
At all costs, they will defend their turf.
Pablo Escobar, drug lord, kept four hippos
on his Colombian estate.
After he died in a shootout, they stayed—
too heavy to move.
Yet crankiness didn't prevent crazed love.
A hundred "cocaine" hippo descendants
float their lives away in Escobar's
Hacienda Napoles, now a park.

I love hippos, despite the havoc
they create, as you love me, my skin rubbed
pink from the bath, another hungry
animal that doesn't belong where she's found,
wet, ill-tempered, digging in.

Waiting
by John Kaprielian

In winter the trees
all arteries arterioles
capillaries rush up
to feed the famished
sky return the life they
drained from the
incandescent summer
sun now dimmed
icy-hearted and low

The days are measured
in crows and jays
and always end half-
done interminable nights
of sleep punctuated by
ellipses exasperation
and dreams of bears

their hibernation broken
pounding at the door
to be let in
for tea.

All this waiting
is getting to me.

Bear
by Fred Gillen Jr.

The almighty dollar
rings a bell and
calls its followers to worship.
All over the world
adherents bow in supplication.
By money's dim sordid light
mountains are destroyed
trees burned
and people starved.
Human wreckage dots the
landscape like happy little clouds
in a Bob Ross painting.
Somewhere in the Catskills
a bear walks along a ledge
and two hikers follow
not considering the danger
waiting where the tracks end,
grateful for the bear's trailblazing.
They'd like to get back to
the marked trail before dark
so they follow
against all advice concerning bears.
They don't find a path.
They find silence and snow,
fir trees and stone.
Maybe they see God

The Morning Dove
by Danny Barbare

So
peaceful
after
the
evening
storm

somewhere
in
the
church
of
a
tree

a
mourning
dove
does
mourn

or
sing
for
its
mate.

I Saw a Million Fireflies
by Tim Brosnan Jr.

I saw a million fireflies dancing overhead
In burning reds and oranges
That vanished at their zenith

The hissing of their mother
Raging down below
Sedated my senses
And in the growing calm
I wondered where their ashes fell

Did they fade into the dark
Like the last whistle of an old man's hum?
Did they rise higher

And higher
Than the moon
And the stars
'Til they became woven into the abyssal void
looming above?

I question whether we are like those fireflies
Born out of warmth both furious and bright
Dancing for eternity
Slipping away into the ether
Or crashing down
Into the dirt

Dragonfly Rite, photo illustration by Christopher Woods

Hope, Cryptic in the Pines
by John Kaprielian

A stand of pines rises between the
stark frozen Hudson and an unnatural
hill that was once landfill, now
a park crossed by paths today
lightly dusted with windblown snow

the walkers and joggers in their
bright attire take no notice of
the tall trees gently swaying
nor do they pay heed when we enter
the copse and stare straight up

binoculars tight to our faces
held with mittened hands this
cold January day that offered
secrets we could not resist
scanning the high boughs we looked

for anything that stood out
but it was all trees and needles
branches gray and green and brown

in the shadows until suddenly they
were not and there high in the

white pine a silent sentinel sat
the glint of golden eyes giving up
his hiding place to us even as
he stretched his body out to
better mimic the ragged branches

ear-tufts arched like a questioning
Brezhnev he waited for us to forget
he was there and go on our way
which we soon did, grinning madly
at our find and heading off for
pastries and hot coffee

Even the well-trod paths of suburbia
can yield unimagined wonders

where owls still perch
so hope does also.

Job Description: Earth Doctor
by Nora Freeman

You must have a background
In healing hopeless cases

We will need you to control with medication
Those who yearn for a Golden Age
That never existed
And are now a danger to self and others

You will be expected to perform
Militarectomies on those nations
Whose armies have grown so swollen

That they are consuming their own body
politics

You will be responsible for
Bringing down the temperature
Of another patient, the Earth
Who stumbled, ablaze, into the ER last night

Your compensation will be
The knowledge
That you have done your part
To leave our children a livable planet

Things Happened, After Terrance Hayes
by Pauli Dutton

Most incidents occurred in the afternoon,
dad at work, brother out playing war,
sister in school.

The woman I called mama had me to herself,
along with a matchbox, cigarettes, and butcher knife.
Things happened.

After she was locked up, grandpa arrived adorned
with hoary face, lion's breath, and wrestler arms.
More things happened.

My fifth summer, sister left me with the pointed teeth
of the man next-door, his son, and a friend.
Things happened then that I never talked about.

For forty years amnesia saved me. When my daughter
turned five, I remembered, and started screaming
the unsayable.

Additional Insurance
by R. Gerry Fabian

Because
the situation
forces him to make a selection,
he reviews what he has chosen
like a butterfly about to land.
He touches
memories that held
various special moments:
a silver-plated ring,
page 173 from *The Catcher In The Rye*,
a pocket Swiss Army knife
with putty and paint
on the handle,
one Betsy Ross dollar
and a short poem
about open spaces.

This is all he needs
except for
the kiss
from the hospital
laser beam.

Senasqua by Susan Obrant
Conte crayon on linen - 30"x24"

Jealousy
by Kathryn P. Haydon

is
a
worm
that
inches
between
friends,
threading
    its
       way among
            good deeds and
      auspicious moments
    until it has
poked
through
to the
other
side
and
no
one
wants
to
eat
the
apple
anymore.

The Shrug
by Kathryn P. Haydon

When will I learn
to remain silent
rather than risk
you stepping

on my heart
when I show you
a dandelion wish
or the plump dewdrop

frosting the rose?
your words are
a shrug
that smushes my joy
and seals my lips.

Never Such a Joy Before
by Sabina Colleran

Never such a joy before
In word order and grammar
He and I; not me and him
What lovely pitter patter
Start with us
The rest comes later
He comes first
As I'm the stater
He and I,
Not me and him,
Surprise ourselves,
Act on a whim.
Lovely chaos;
Perfectly framed
In syntax strong
And sentences tamed.
She and I
Not me and her
We love the sound
of sound grammar.

Birthday Excursion
by Alan Feldman

It's a raw day to visit a garden
but this is the day we have. The Latin
inscription on the orangerie says
"If there's a heaven on earth, this
is it." A kind of ancient blurb.
And every fountain is in memory of
someone. Every tree has a label
with its name, like the Russian fir,
that looks sad, like a bushy exile,
with little pencil-like pendants
clipped to its drooping, shaggy arms,
soaked in fox urine, to keep
the deer off. It gets on my fingers.

When she asks what I'm thinking I say
I'm hoping soap can take this off.
How did I get so banal? I bore even me.
And it's her birthday. I'm sure
I used to be better company. Back then
if we had a spare hour we'd jump into bed.
Now I like to take a nap. Or maybe
nap to music. Put on some jazz.
Ill-starred Bill Evans with Scott LaFaro
who died so young, just days after
his fingers slid so suggestively over
his bass, as if a bass could hum
like a happy, busy person. A large person
the size of a tree. The way a Russian fir
might hum. Yes, I'd lie down and listen
to these two commune with each other
telepathically, like a long-married couple,
playing at the Village Vanguard
amidst tinkling forks and laughter.
If I do nap, she'll guess I don't want to visit
the city galleries or the museum tonight.
This garden is quite enough for me.

All those plaques. So many for the dead:
An urn. A cupid. A fountain. A walkway.
A gate. Really, I'd lie down right here
a monument to myself. But it's her birthday.
And love is more mysterious than the periwinkle
ground cover that keeps recurring.

Tomorrow I'll say no, and yet again no.
A garden? City galleries? The museum? Too much.
But tonight I'll say, Let's go. And we will.
To everything she wants to see. Though the wind
is more like March, and the orange trees
they've moved outside will be shivering all night,
even their bright globes of gold.

a word or two
will do
wonders...

what a day for an idea,
what an idea for a day

The Cicerone
by Fred Pollack

This was the corner. I took out
the photo to confirm. For their own reasons,
the communists then the West had left
the cobblestones, but rooflines were the same,
and the old church tower. The figure
in a white shirt with a righteous bestial snarl,
holding whatever club had come to hand,
must have died decades since, surrounded by grandkids.
Other figures blurred; even the dead
seemed to have hurried into bloody heaps.
The Germans who arrived the next day
were pleased by local vigor but not its disorder.
A Starbucks that had replaced
whatever had replaced the tailor shop
afforded a view unavailable then.

And of course he was there, as always,
a stranger but accepted by the natives
of all these places. Old, respectable,
here doubtless for good reason, pleasant
but unapproachable even to local gangs.
My drink went on his endless tab,
his suit and features merged with shadow,
and he said, as he does everywhere:
"I didn't plan it. I intended
space as the distance crossed in an embrace,
time as the joyful tension needed
to solve a problem, as in art or math.
You can say I was uninformed,
and that it was long ago, though nothing is."

Bulldog
by Kevin Pilkington

On 93rd Street there's a hill between
2nd and 3rd Avenues, one of the few in the city
steeper than any you built over the years
and only have yourself to blame.
At its foot, more near the ankle, there
is a fruit cart with grapefruits the size
of softballs, apples the color of a kiss
you never plan forgetting, blueberries
that belong in cereal and melons you can
push your fingers in and bowl strikes
every time.

As you walk up your right leg starts
to cramp as if a traffic jam is in it
and forces you to lean against a tree
like it's your best friend with years
of bark between you and stretch your leg
until cars start moving again and so
do you.

Halfway up a young guy with pink
hair and an eagle tattoo that landed on
his arm, is selling old vinyl records held in
milk crates in front of a small park.
You stop to flip through them then stop
again just to look at the Blonde on Blonde
album with the large photo of Dylan
on the cover. It's the one where he looks like
Lord Byron who you would have read
more in college if he played guitar,
sang his poems in front of a backup band
or did an occasional cover of Coleridge's
Kubla Khan with Maceo Parker on sax
taking it to the bridge.

When you reach the top of the hill
and look across 2nd Avenue there is a small
white sports car that you could drive
back to when you were a kid and what
you are going through now was years away.
It looks a lot like the bulldog you had
then. His face was a wrinkled shirt
and always came to you to be hugged since
at 4'8" and 50 pounds you were
what love looked like.

Before you turn to go back to an empty
apartment you make sure no one
sees you whistle at it, then quickly turn
and start walking down the hill hoping
it will follow you, all the way home.

Pop Art Calling, by Moydan, Michael McKee

Phil and Pete
by Fred Pollack

On the terrace, on the bench
around the water feature,
or on rainy nights in the rec room,
they share a certain rank. Both widowers
who never remarried; both,
still, evidently,
well-off; kids visit with grandkids.
Phil wins at cards; Pete loses
deliberately to Ruth,
who is secretly glad, everyone knows,
of an extra twenty bucks. Phil
patient but silent when
she elegizes her career
in summer stock in Hartford; Pete
cheerfully feeding her questions
she's delighted to answer and has answered often.
He's also attentive to Mrs. H,
who has forgotten more, but she gravitates
towards Phil. Who provides
not anecdotes but facts
to Paul, Herb, Dan, when nightly they
discuss their wars. When someone stops
appearing for meals, and eventually
the ambulance comes, Pete isn't
very good; he has been seen to weep
in corners; but always says a few words
later, even for the difficult Carol,
and, that June, Mrs. H.
Phil, in contrast, visits such people
in their rooms and at the hospital;
someone, through an open door,
once saw him speaking quietly and seriously.
One night they had found themselves
alone in adjoining armchairs in the rec room.
"I feel sorry for women," said Pete.
"They've been given a raw deal."
"I grieve for mankind as a whole," said Phil
in his usual subdued way.
And although both sensed an affinity,
they didn't like each other very much.

So I Think I'm Going
by Ken Pobo

to stop it, this falling in
love, I do it too easily, I can
be walking down the street

on my way to Wawa for coffee,
and there the latest you are,
you don't really know me,

maybe we went to high school
together, even had that hideous
geometry teacher who called

school a circumference,
I wave at you and you look
like I'm one more gas pump,

I'm sending desire
to reform school, he only
gets me in trouble, but

I might want him to
return, I crave to be
in love like a baseball card

flapping in a bike wheel, round
and round, even though I know
the wheel will stop turning.

Peeking by Anne Maizianne
Acrylics/mixed media on canvas - 30" x 30" x 1"

I'll go to Hell when I die, I'm ready
by Gale Acuff

now, not to die but to go to Hell, there's
a difference and when I've figured out what
it is then maybe I'll actually
get to go to Heaven instead but if
I do then I'll probably walk up to
God and challenge His authority, say
Maybe you're the Creator and maybe
you're in charge but maybe it's time for fair
and free elections--let somebody else
take a crack at managing chaos and
saying it's good *and while I'm about it*
this business about Jesus being your
son but at the same time you yourself, that
needs to stop. And then maybe I'll wake up.

I love everybody but I have no
by Gale Acuff

choice because if I don't I don't get to
go to Heaven and live with Jesus or
at least God when I die--no, I go to
Hell to burn forever, at least the folks
at our church do and I'm one of 'em though
just ten years old but I won't always be,
I'll be old enough to someday to sin like
a sailor but then if I don't learn to
love everybody else, me included,
no matter how rotten then I'll wind up
in Hell anyway--whatever happened
to Jesus dying for your sins so you'll
be forgiven? My teacher tells me that
especially in death there's a future.

Nobody lives forever unless they
by Gale Acuff

croak says my Sunday School teacher but she
didn't say *croak*, I'm ten years old so that
word belongs to me but anyway to
get eternal life I have to die and
God moves in mysterious ways, that's from
some song or maybe even the Bible
or Shakespeare or Stan Lee but anyway
I won't get to live forever and I
should've known there would be a catch unless
I die first and that's what's called *religion*
and I'm not sure I like it, you'd think that
to gain everything you wouldn't need to
lose something, especially a something
that's all. That's just what's dumb about grownups.

Stars and Stripes <u>by Red Sagalow</u>
Drypoint Etching and Watercolor - 5" x 6.5"

Pulling In
by Rachael Ikins

Strung beads of words, rafts and murders of words,
crows harass an owl caught visible, napping in daylight.
Words shout from pages, pick me! Pick me! pull you in
before you know it you're drowning. Word-weapons lance
deeper than any knife, scars of words permanent and stab
the heart. Words egg on the disenfranchised, words whip up
a mob, gun-toting mob POW! POW! POW! of words, January sixth.

The pow-er of lied words, lie's irresistible unthinking lure, the obdurate
ignorance of self-righteousness. Words weight, texture, granite's substance,
skin my knee and blood, like words, weeps between my laced fingers.
Waiting for snow to fall, waiting to see if this year winter will be too warm,
Greenland melting, Antarctica calves too many icebergs, ocean desalinates
and sucks Florida under while I wait for Iceland's Orca to siphon carbon dioxide
from the atmosphere, to frack it deep into bedrock below. Waiting for stag horn

coral to take hold, waiting in a bayou canoe for an extinct/maybe not woodpecker,
waiting for when white skin won't matter. I lie in bed at 2:00 a.m.
waiting for that mouse to start gnawing the wall behind
bathroom cabinets, waiting for random fireworks on the river
to burn out, dogs to shut up. I am waiting, inevitably,
a silent moment's pause,
for my heart to beat.

Awaiting Warm Air
by Lynda Wolfe Coupe

I'm awaiting the warm air
of spring
that breathes like hope

a new atmosphere
for a new season
to banish the vapors of winter

I want to inhale energy
inflate tired lungs
revive a languid heart

I think I see the birds
quicken to nature's vernal song
but perhaps it's only fancy

perhaps yearning makes its own truth
perhaps wanting becomes a world
perhaps warm air inspires poetry

Our Lack of Faith in Seed
by William Doreski

Even when the air is still the wind
is plotting to undress itself
in public, exposing everything.

You worry that too little sky
upholsters us from the bump
and grind of coming nuclear war.

You doubt that the shadows cast
on brickwork in ancient mill towns
can smooth the rough to ease us

through afternoons that narrow down
to the essential and fatal point.
The lyric expressions strangers

don when we slurp our tea aloud
remind us how simple we are.
The days weep into spring when

the last gobbets of snow withdraw,
the crows rattle like scrap metal,
and budding maples rebuke us

for our lack of faith in seed.
The wind lurks in the background,
slightly offstage. Its tempers

chime with ours although we hate
to admit it. The vacancies
prolong themselves in brown tones

like old photographs. No one cares
about such detritus, but the sighs
creeping from things in boxes
stored in dusty attics shame us
and encourage the wind to pick up
where it left off, and finish us.

Winter Sunning by Sharon Kullberg
Oil on wood - 6" x 6"

An die Entschwundene Flora
by Jack Harvey

Those sweet days;
young spring;
the robin,
like an adventure,
sings his
dull return.

Those sweet nights;
your ruff of hair
touched,
wet with promise.

Beyond the call
of blood, the stars
rain down
favor or disfavor;
one.

Tears after
sweet congress
distill drop by
drop,
touch my flesh
not like drops
of rain,
but the eternal tears,
blank heaven's
reward for the
living.

Listen to me,
querida,
sought and
found;
this sweet time

a moment
will last,
and then pass
you and me
and all we were.
So let us love
these days;
young spring's
but a mortal time
and no return
for you or me
will ever be.

Under the Tree
by Diarmuid Maolala

and yes, it's cold out
in the spill of this sunlight
but we've captured some
summer and put it there,
under the tree.
spent saturdays gathering
various objects, not because
we love objects,
but because
we love people

and we don't think
(I don't think) about getting
things, either; we think

about other people,
and seeing them
get. I can't help it –
I love it –
red wine with white meat
and long conversations,
the coat of december
like ivy on walls.

it's what makes us
different than animals.
it's what makes us the same
as animals.

Schnouff in Repose
by Kelly Harris

With head upon hand,
for once I gaze upon her, this beauty,
undetected.
How is it that her sensitive senses
have not discovered me?
Her side heaves gently, quivering slightly, falling
as the breaths of sleep work their rhythms
and tiny twitches of her limbs beat a delicate counterpoint.
She has been with me eight years now
and I hope she lives another ten,
this companion well met in my time of need.
When I saw her so composed on a chill night
in that cage on the street that means New York,
I knew she was the one I sought.
And so we drift through another night
as inky Winter settles upon us,
two dreamers, fragile creatures,
an aging man and his November cat.

Answers
by Marcy B. Freedman

My son is upset
Each time I insist
That I have no answers

He wants answers
But I refuse
To give him any

I see the look
On his face
As he hears my plea

Of ignorance

Life has taught me
Things, but
I will not share them.

Why burden my son
With the few truths
That I have found?

They are too painful.

I'd rather deal with the pain
That I cause my son
When pretending to know

Nothing.

Man in the Moon
by Diane Funston

I'll plant a pink dogwood tree
next week,
but not for my children.
My sons will sell this house
after I'm gone to grave.
They'll want none of my collections.

My garden may be plowed under,
returned to wasteful unimaginative lawn,
fertilized,
manicured,
Round-Upped.

My rocks and minerals,
two big glass cabinets full
will be Ebayed and auctioned,
to the highest bidder
despite the eons to form
and my years to collect them.

The glass curio of Mexican folk art.
Día de los Muertos
Catrinas and Catrines
skulls and fantasy animals
will cross the border of my home
to be scattered to thrift stores
along with never-fading Talavera.

Will the man in the moon still be there,
along with lunar art,
sculptures of moon-mother
received with love
gifts from friends who knew my spirit,
or the polar bears, spirit animal
of my drive for solitude, sex, and strength.

Books will be in the hands of strangers,
all the poetry of knowns and unknowns,
all their passionate words,
brave insertions, the literature
from brave new worlds
gathering dust instead of discussion
at the local Goodwill.

So I'll plant the pink dogwood next week.
Into my lush front garden
devoid of pedestrian lawn,
amidst fruit trees and vegetable plots,
succulents and Redwoods.
I'll live my life in the pleasure
of my curated joy,
my lust for travel and adventure.
Until I too am plowed under,
forever facing upward.
Will the man in the moon still be there?

Poetry, the writer's plight
by Kelly Harris

poetry is so bare, so spare, so exposed,
each line vulnerable to the critical eye and the scourge of reason—
each word cavils at the demands upon it,
each word must swim or fly, or sizzle or sting—
cliché, triteness, commonplaces will abort the fantasy,
cast the reader into the pit of banality,
the weary, dreary dullness of daily life—
and tone, how to serve it?
be dissonant, but avoid pain,
one must earn consonance,
find the suitable cadence;
and better to avoid rhyme,
in this time unless,
of course, it's internal

it's more pathetic than pretentious
that the drudges of Calliope should favor process as a subject,
but it's their familiar, their bane,
a little pity, please?

Lover/Loved?
by Jack Powers

I choose to be the lover, not the loved
or am I just nursing bruises from the shove-
and-be-shoved jostle of our daily ties,
the hold and chafe that keep us equalized?

Tomorrow, might I say that I'm the latter?
A good night's sleep, a kiss, some morning
     chatter
and my wounded heart will grow warm and full,
love's tides abate and ease the push and pull?

And when an old friend says, We never fought,
After her husband's sudden split, I'm caught
Between shock and sorrow. She never stopped
to shake all the vinegar to the top?

When they made nice, they should have made a
     fuss.
Sometimes it's selfishness that's saving us.

Heart Trouble
by Cynthia Andersen

Put your hand over your heart,
Feel the miraculous muscle pump
A sea of blood to every body part.
Under stress, fear, and if you jump,
The primordial rhythm quickens,
But still the heart will pump.
Few nerves there are; pain can't pierce,
Yet when love fails we call it heartache,
Heartbreak and the pain is fierce.
Heart is of body and mind:
Only purified souls can perceive love, Plato taught mankind,
But hearts fail to understand, to see, to care.
When one meets a kindred spirit and love fails
It seems so unfair.
The doctor listens to the heart through a stethoscope,
A friend through the telephone
Both are called upon to give some hope.
The doctor hears two sounds; first and second, echoing again and again.
The friend hears three: outrage, anger and pain.
I want you to hear my heart's pain through verse,
And if you listen with YOUR heart
Perhaps you can hear the cry of the Universe.

Post Hurricane Irene, photo by Tom Tarnowski

Faith Ringgold by Ellen Elchlepp
Oil on Belgian Linen - 18"x18"

Remains
by Vera Salter

I am glad that Sleepy Hollow
Cemetery has a green burial
section with a view of the river.

My husband is claustrophobic.
He told me years ago
he wants to be cremated.

My mother said she wanted
to be buried in a plain pine box.
A surprise to my sister who expected

her to be cremated at Hoop Lane
Crematorium like our father
and everyone in North London.

My sister had no choice in Orthodox
Jerusalem. She was wrapped in a shroud
and sealed in a concrete drawer.

If I am around when my husband is cremated,
I will place his urn under the bench he erected
for his brother next to his parents' graves.

My will still says I am to be cremated,
but I cringe at being incinerated.
There is comfort in returning to the earth.

Whence?
by George Robinson

I am from fifth floor walk ups
From cockroaches in the cupboards
And dumbwaiters in the walls.

From TV dinners on snack tables

From The Ed Sullivan Show and Bonanza

And "I'd give it a ten because you can dance
to it, Mr. Clark."

I am from two-sewer stickball
And stoopball
Always armed with hangers to fish out
Spaldings from the sewers.

I am from blankets on tar beach
Where pigeons coo and opera singers serenade
In the courtyard below for tossed coins.

I'm from Ad Deum qui laetificat
And "Bless me Father, for I have sinned."

and Sunday Latin Mass

where the boys twitched in rows
while the girls bowed their laced heads
pretending to
pray for the Conversion of Russia.

I'm from fifteen cent subway rides
Avoiding the strap hangers to stand
Wide legged at the front window
Slaloming down the tracks with the conductor.

My scrapbook languishes with

Faded photos, newspaper clippings and
homecoming football rosters

That see the light of day once a decade,

But their nostalgic dust comforts me nightly.

The Dry Stone Walls of Innis Oírr
by Stephen M. Jacoby

They are everywhere
Defining tiny fields
Climbing hills
Lining narrow lanes
Terracing below the castle
Surrounding three cows
Enclosing a rusted tractor
Skeleton

I can walk among them for hours
I can stand before them
(Even now in my mind)
And gaze upon patterns of the rocks

I think I see the hands of many hundreds
Over a thousand years,
Each distinct and different

Like handwriting, here print,
There cursive. Obsessive:
Neat horizontal rows
Topped by perpendiculars,

All parallel and similar;
Impulsive: stones leaning
This way and that, wildly varying
In size and shape, hasty;

A story teller: the stones
Not quite parallel so they seem
To sway as read from side to side
Like music; an extrovert: his mark

Is made tall, of heavy, jagged slabs
Leaning as if each had been lifted high
And dropped in place; the complex
Planner with planned pattern

Like a weaver's, alternating
Verticals and horizontals,
In four ranks. Here, a break in the wall
Has been filled by a different hand,

In a different time. The broken
Rhythm tells it all. Stones weathering
And slipping from their ranks are older;
A few dressed stones in another wall

Shout new. Almost no one is here now.
The fields, walled to keep soil in
And flying sand out, are mostly weeds,
Cows and sheep are few.

So many once built; so many have gone;
So few remain. Left behind:
A library of stone.

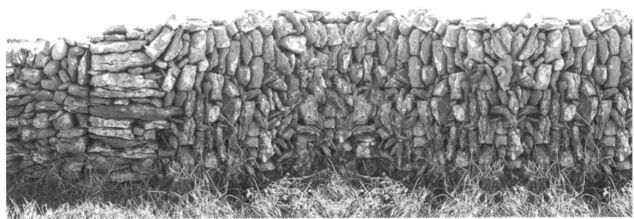

House with Girl Standing
by Laurie Steinhorst
Image transfer, pencil, and cotton thread
on paper - 26" x 20"

Orange Dresses
by Laurie Steinhorst
Image transfer, pencil, and ink
on paper 12" x 9"

Memory of Treasured Worlds
by Wendy K. Mages

We gather our supplies, Wonder Bread, Elmer's Glue, and food coloring. We begin to create our clay. Tearing the bread into small bits and mixing in Elmer's Glue, my sister and I knead the mixture in our hands, its yeasty scent filling the air. When the dough is completely smooth and glossy, we divide it into sections. Leaving one lump uncolored, we blend a few drops of food coloring into each of the other sections, creating soft pastels: rosy pinks, robin egg blues, and sunshine yellows. The blades of grass take extra food coloring to turn the clay the perfect shade of green.

Once we have created our full palette of colors, we begin to sculpt. We create miniature mushrooms, snails, turtles, flowers, and blades of grass. With a drop or two of glue, we affix each of these tiny sculptures to one of the rocks we've collected, the craggier the rock the better. When our fairy landscapes are complete, we let them dry overnight. In the morning, we spray them with lacquer to preserve them forever.

*****

Like memories of times past, most artful expressions of youth rarely make it to forever. Over the years, and through multiple moves, our whimsical landscapes were lost or discarded, the flotsam and jetsam of childhood. Yet, one of the more intricate of these magical worlds was safeguarded. Loved and protected, my mom cherished this little garden of miniscule mushrooms, fanciful flowers, and teensy turtles, keeping it safe until she, too, was but memory….

Strawberry Daze
by Jess L Parker

We pluck fresh strawberries—
their little red noses bursting with seeds,
on the verge of multiplication. These berries

are meant for pie and although we cannot, we try
to hide our tart, pink fingers, drenched in juice.

Our puckered tongues hover behind gaps in
baby teeth, each wobbly grin giving us
away.

Black-Eyed Susan
by Jenna Lynn Good

bats flapping
across a dusk-field. star light, star
bright—the one-eyed half-
moon saw you kiss me.

texture of hay, color of
honey, black leaves: frayed
shadows scatter like broken
glass through broken blinds.

pressed
petals, touch and turn
to dust in your hands.

Lamplight
by Janet McCann

A flash and the tube light darkens.
I sit at the table, perplexed.
Is it the tube itself, or perhaps
The current up there. The fan
Does not work either. I sigh,

Find two lamps in the dusty garage,
Brush off spiderwebs and bugs.
The old bulbs glow when I plug in
The cords, and two golden circles
Intersect on my desk. I like this light.

It is mandorla, the eye of the soul,
Mandorla, almond, the shape of the
Shared space. Or is it Vesica Piscis,
The fish in the overlap, from Euclid,
Sacred geometry taken by Christians?

Or two young lovers walking in the rain,
Side by side, under their umbrellas?
Or maybe just part of a Venn diagram,
Waiting for the third circle,
The one which will clarify everything?

Freedom Tower, photo by Pam Zicca

You were the first one and now I have the history of the open
by Elena Botts

We met at Union station, I feel like. We did not meet in Union Station. It was Dupont. I'm sorry, I get the series of events all wrong. I go through them in my mind and simply. All the places we went to, we went to at least twice, and then it was over.

You were looking for your backpack because you had left it on the metro, you said. This was the first thing you said to me. Before I was walking with you, you were another stranger standing outside the station. "I lost my backpack," you said again, "Do you think there's a number?"

"Like Lost and Found? Yeah, you should call."

I told you I had poor vision, so I might not see you, and that you would have to come to me. I had a John Ashbery poem "stuck in my head": so I thought, 'You must come to me all golden and pale. Like the dew or the air...' You thought I was blind. I thought nothing of meeting you, I was merely. I was trying to get home. But there you were, small against the escalator, among the people who together made real the word "among".

I was exhausted then and am exhausted now. You and I went to the station. No, see, I am getting it all wrong. We went to my friends, a private party in the Organization of American States, but the smaller building next to it where they pack and transport the artworks. There, my friends and their skateboards. There, we unwrapped the CDs and with that easy familiarity, which somehow you also became ingratiated in, we put the CDs in their wrappings, their cases. I might've said aloud that this album was written in March after a February that tore at my heart. It was about blood, and horses, and all-consuming guilt, sins that even the Madonna could not endure. I had watched Andrei Rublev too many times, and I felt like him in that way, I felt that each person I knew in some intimate way would become burdened by me, and that in the end each relationship was a dead horse, a stallion I had recklessly slaughtered. I would watch the blood from the neck. A clean cut like in that movie, which movie? The other one, with the butcher and his daughter. Blood from the neck, and the sound as the neck falls empty, and the blood falls away, to the floor. You look like the one who made me feel this way, guilty. You also are small and a few years younger than I, but you are not mean as they were, unsure of themself to the point of cruelty. They were named C., and went to school in Massachusetts and I had spent few February days with them, cold and without appetite, in appreciation of their form, but feeling missing, as though I were not wanted there after all, and did not mind leaving, only minded being wrongly invited at all. I had felt, with them, I had opened something unopenable, and suffered as I was meant to, for this reason, with someone who could not reckon with vulnerability. I had overstepped, and now was stained with the force of my own small invasion. I felt ungentle, terrible. I had wished then never to be born, or at least to no longer trip over certain contexts. These days, I remembered this mark but still intended to give, more carefully. I was easy with my friends.

My friends and I after went to sleep on my mother's floor. I had stopped paying rent at my old flat and then I was kicked out of my father's as well. He had abusive tendencies, I told him. He was a sweet man, bearded and blue-eyed, and full of hesitations, and yet he could not handle himself. He controlled the world around him to the extent he could, until the world shrank to a few cabinets, some vegetables, and the half in, half out of this world girlfriend of his, shivering away and forever weakened, at a loss, following her brain surgery. Though I had never felt at home. I was tired too of living anywhere. I ached for the hills, for solace and a respite from the living world. I was glad to see my friends. D. eyed me over breakfast, talking about her new boyfriend while N. skated the length of the neighborhood. When the time came for them to leave, N. stood saying, "Can I hug you?"

This time I agreed. I went back to DC, back to school and important men to walk the dark monuments with and speak of futures, how I hoped for these futures. We turned at the end of Farragut Square, and the last man bid me adieu in his Ukrainian accent, his tall silhouette ungainly against the backdrop of ambulances rushing down K. Street.

"Where do you wanna go? I have Chinese leftovers." You said this twice. "I have Chinese leftovers." I thought of the word leftovers. I didn't know where to go, so I got on the train with you and we got off at Union. It was grand, empty, but also farcical - there were some preparations underway, stars and stripes projected tackily against the fine marble. I waltzed around, taking a book of comics left by some missionaries, inspecting the little characters as they proclaimed, in all capital letters, their torments, before, of course, the good lord stepped in. I tore out pages of the book, and with the gum you offered me, stuck small unrelated images throughout the station. You were giggly, soft. We reached a Starbucks. I tried to steal a banana for you, but an alarm system came on, and I scattered. You walked blithely away, and I rejoined you, until we found some chairs to sit on and you offered me Chinese. I had bits and pieces.

"Do you eat anything besides candy and small pieces of bread?" you asked me, and I did not answer, for once, embarrassed.

You had small dark curved eyes, eyes that seemed to fall upon a different outline, they had a significant contour, they signified. Your nose and mouth - you were cute. Your hair was out now, black and Jewish and wild. I said, "I like your hair. It's different than yesterday. "

"It is so much. Ugh. I had it up. It was less all over the place then."

An employee comes over, asks if she can stack our chairs. You are apologizing. We leave, get on the train together, passing a homeless man sleeping in the doorway. The light inside the metro is bright, fluorescent. You explain that you have come from West Virginia but have lived many places, and are staying in DC.

"You do know the metro closes at 11? I might go home soon. Where do you want to go?"

You don't know. We are here, or here, but then the next moment happens, the train leaves. There is only one need. It is to stay together long enough to keep talking, to finish this conversation. I feel as though everyone in the train is listening, all these anonymous DC people, as you tell of how you were sent away to school in Arizona because you were depressed in high school, how later you dropped out of McGill, traveled to Peru, Morocco. You say your friends are crazy because they were the crazy girls at the special school, and you didn't like the sad ones, like you. Your friends are scattered around now, at their respective colleges and pursuits.

"They were boring," you say. "I later caught up with the crazy ones and had a promiscuous phase."

You have a hard time with your mother, your step-dad runs a men's group and is overly enthusiastic about interventions. Your father is wealthy, and more reasonable. We are at the end of the line now, confused, but still together. We walk towards my car, and I drive it gently through the barricade to avoid paying the parking fee. You sit there. I sit there. It is cold outside, hot in the car.

"What are our options?" I say aloud. "We could sleep at my mom's, but it would be hard. Only floor space, and she's reluctant..."

"Wanna go to West Virginia?" You laugh. I have responsibilities in DC, tomorrow, though. We drive to my mom's, and she emerges, surprised, in a white bathrobe, before returning back upstairs to her newspaper.

You are looking through the books. "Your mom, is she a therapist? So is mine," you say. We are arranging our things on the floor, rearranging them.

"You know what?", you say. I look up. "If you drive," I say, "I'll go wherever you take me - as long as you bring me back tomorrow." You have your bag in hand. "Let's go."

We are back in the car, long miles, deep darkness, getting deeper in the hills, until we enter a ridge in the earth, a darkness that splits wide open, and the small town lights are winking. You drive the Prius up the hill, and it struggles over the steep slope. Here is a house built like a dome, complete with a garden, warmed from the inside by a wood stove. A small cat greets us. You let the dog outside.

This was the first time. You smoke a cigarette on the porch at the top of the dome, both of us staring at the impossible circle of light around the full autumnal moon. We bend over the space heaters in a house that is still cold, in this sudden winter cold that has only just begun.

In the dark green sweater, your back forms a crooked curve, one that I cannot help but notice, and think - and there is something beautiful. You are warming your hands.

I am at a loss. "I wanna say something," I say, "But I don't know - if I should say it."

"What, what is it," a statement more than a question. Your dark, almost black eyes, small and with this penetrating light.

"I think..." I stretch it out, bend also to the heater, back, away again, sit on the edge of the bed, "I have a crush."

"Oh," you say, "I do too." And I go on, and you repeat all these things after me, as though they are normal and we both know them. I love especially how you say 'I know', as though everything I say is really just a reiteration of something that I needn't have said, because really, you already know. We retire to our separate rooms, and I awake in sunlit confusion, only to have you drive me back to school, to the important men, because really, they hadn't happened before - I've been so confused - and I was so relieved to get away from the capital the second time, it was bliss to stretch the mind awake away from the petty affairs of the world, and no longer tend to my appearance in a world of suits.

You met me at Union Station. This was the second time. We planned to go to New York, but I did not want to any longer. "I just got back from there four days ago," I told you as we sat in a row of empty seats by the Amtrak. A man came to sit behind us and I wondered if he had come to sit precisely behind us just to listen in to our conversation. Or maybe I said this as we walked through the double set of doors out onto the metro, this time passing no one, because the homeless man who had been sleeping there before was gone. We were on the metro for awhile, and I still felt as though everyone were listening - when suddenly, you began to cry.

Or, you didn't actually cry, but to me you said, "I think I'm going to cry..."

We got off the train, you, running delighted to a bus that turned out to be out of service. "Well," you said, resigned, sitting on the bus stop bench, "We could wait until 8:26 or walk for 20 minutes."

"Let's walk," I said. As we crossed the parking lot, I wondered aloud what had made you so sad. We were in a neighborhood now. No clarity for you, but houses. Now I was meeting your mother - small, beatific, full of endless energy, too-bright eyes. Your step-dad: rumpled, attractive, young, unshaven. A hand extended.

"It's so good that you're going to Berkeley Springs," your mother said giddily, every word like an interjection, "Keep the home fires burning! And you'll see the queen! Has E. met the queen?"

"The queen...," I say, out loud, "Oh, you mean the cat."

Your step-dad wandered out of the shower, clutching shampoo. "In the bathroom," he said, "There's poo, and there's shampoo." This proclamation was met with a positive response from your mother, and a tired look from you to me.

We were in the car again - again, again. And then we were petting the cat in your room, under the skylight, the full moon. The cat sits between us, stretching, grey, friendly green eyes, always going and then returning. "Should I ask?" I say, as though to myself, or to you.

"Ask?"

I am uncertain, but find myself in this sudden insurmountable. There are snatches of you, of your bright dark eyes, which are really so soulful or full of something, doubtless, the way you bite your lip in hesitance, your wild black curls. You are small, and made of something, something very true.

Two nights in a row, under the moon, like geese in a row as they move in formation, south, on this soon-to-be-winter day. There is a nothing to us, simply in your hair, and you, full of sweet looks. You have what look like acne scars, soft, impossible, rose-colored. The you of you. You are full of care, you are familiar to tuck into my shoulder blade, and hold the mind. I evade you, but return. It is kind, I think, and you are you, without explanation. I think about your finite bends and sleepy endlessness. You laugh at me when I try to count your vertebrae. I am happy, then.

And then I am tired. In between this, somehow, is a day, full of a trip to the coffee shop that your mother owns, and a flat trip to the grocery store, where, in a panic, we try to buy enough to use the coupon your mother gave us. You know everyone in town, their daughters and husbands and wives. You say hello in a different voice, but still thoughtful. You show me some baby teeth your mother had embedded in a mosaic wall of stone. You hate the mural that the man painted on the side of the store: inexplicably, he thought it wise to include both Iwo Jima and Yoda, side by side. Such is the American way, he must've thought. We are sandwiched between old-timers in motorized carts. I wake, feeling, now, totally at a loss, totally sunlit, totally over. You try to come into the spare room where I sleep but I turn away. I can hardly muster the words to say: "You woke me up." You apologize and retreat to yours. I listen to music alone in my room all morning and then start messing with my synthesizer. Later, I find you, and you sit on the edge of the bed. Neither of us knows what to do. I am wordless, I want to be alone, I no longer have words with you. I lie back, my mind is emptied. With you, I cannot speak. I have already said enough.

"My crazy mentor has invited us to brunch," you say, "But I couldn't find the car keys in time so now she texted me to just come over. She's a dominatrix."

"You're interested in sex work?"

"No, I just want to know how she influences people. I think it's interesting. Or, well, I admire it. I want to be able to do that." I look at you for a moment, thoughtless.

"Okay, let's go."

We are on a winding country road, in the hills that remind me of the hills I so deeply long for, back in upstate New York. I am plaintive, nonverbal, staring at the winter trees cast in rich evening light.

Cast in gold. I am afraid I have Midas' touch, that I will hurt you or otherwise be bad for you in some way. I am also tired, so tired. I wonder again whether we will part as friends, when this all fades, or if we will always hold this sweetness like a note in the air that goes and goes inaudibly, now that the moment is done, now that I have shown you my true appreciation. "What else is there to say - I have nothing to say-" Or if this is one of the last rides I will take with you, you driving my car, focused on the curve of the road, that slight wrinkle of concentration forming around your eyes. I think, we will be better in middle age, you and I. It will be better then. Or maybe when we part, that is the last look I will be granted into your little world, your young wise eyes. I want, more than anything, to be good to you, and it is no matter whether I am here or there, so long as I do that - and that we are now, still together, for this fourth day, is indisputable, and the long hour weighs upon my chest as I wonder if this is where I should be, at this moment, in relation to you, or if this is a stolen hour too far - I cannot think with you here. I must go.

You sit with S., the dominatrix, in her small trailer-like house, oppressive wood paneling and two hefty brown dogs play-fighting, and you smoke a joint together and she does her make-up. "This one's his mom," you say, pointing to one dog as the other lunges. S. likes to talk about boundaries, is always congratulating herself or others for taking a stand. She has an impenetrable face, and is always watching us. Earlier you told me that you had slept at her house once - thought nothing transpired - and you saw that she texted one of her partners: "Just woke up next to a beautiful young woman half my age!"

"So much for boundaries," I say. Someone else might stick to you in this house, to see if she poses any real threat to you, but I am doubtful and figure, always, that you know what you are doing. She invites us to the bar but you decline, and we walk back to the car.

I forget this part. On the way there we had to stop in someone's drive-way. I had asked if you thought we should be just friends soon. I said, romance for me is a means to friendship, and is short lived in itself, it is just a moment of uncovering before the real thing. Or perhaps it is loss. It is both, really.

"We should wait until we see each other again and then talk then," you say, which I find judicious.

"If we do," I say. "Though I'd like to be friends awhile."

"Me too." You pause, with a hand on the mirror, "I think that the longevity of this depends on it."

Soon after, you start crying again, which is when we have to stop the car, and all I can hear is the sound of the willow tree scraping, even whispering against the car window, and I hold your face with my hand until you silently turn the car back on.

"We never did find my backpack," you say. "I wish I hadn't lost it, though I have my wallet and phone I miss the journals - I was working on a writing project."

On the way back from S.'s house, we don't know where to go, again. You suggest your house, the dome, and then ask if we should just after all, part ways. We are both so ready, and sad, and eager for the impending loss. You park the car in the darkness at the base of the hill, crying again. I kiss your face.

"I'm going to smoke a cigarette," you say, opening the car door and I stay inside, leave you alone out there in the space between the warehouses, thinking of the day before when I took one of many photos, this one of you climbing onto a railcar as the sun set over the train yard.

You get back into the car. No words but steady miles. I am wondering if we forgot something. I think of the space heater I left on, I think of the dog and the cat, of the groceries left in the fridge. I cannot break this silence. You start to get out of the car when we reach your house. I pull you back. I hope that no one is looking out at us on this neighborhood street. I get up and walk around to the driver's seat, while you get your bag from the backseat.

"Is that all?" I ask, indicating your bag.

"Yes" you say, and I open the driver's side door, turn the key quickly as you walk away.

Flowering by Lynne Friedman
watercolor - 4"x6"

When the Whip Comes Down
by Mario Duarte

It is almost the end of summer, a Saturday. Mama and my hermana Aleta are off shopping for new school clothes. Aleta dances all the way to our junky car and blows me a big fat wet raspberry goodbye. What a pendeja!

Not long after they took off papi called his friend Mr. Teal, a man who use to work with papi at the shop and invites him over for "a few drinks."

Right before, Mr. Teal arrives, Papa says to me, "If you're quiet" I could sit with them at the kitchen table until I finished snacking on some peanuts and a Pepsi.

"I'll be quiet, promise." I am an ear on the wall. Quietly listening.

"Just one more drink," Mr. Teal said. His watery eyes are bloodshot, nose sunset red, and cheeks flusher than lava snaking into the sea.

"Of course, my good man," replies papi grandly as he refills Mr. Teal's empty shot class with more Seagram's 7. The crown on top of the 7 on the bottle's label slightly off kilter.

Papi licks his lips. "Just another to wet the whistle, hey?" he asks. Mr. Teal chuckles.

"Say, that reminds me," Mr. Teal says. "The last time I whistled it was because this crazy man down the street cracking a whip on his driveway."

"No kidding" says papi. "When I was chico, a boy living in the rancho, the men used whips to herd the cattle." Papi's glassy eyes blink into the bottom of his empty shot glass.

"That's nothin" slurred Mr. Teal. "My old man use a whip to scare the hell out of us. If we did somethin' he didn't like, he would take out this old black leather whip and crack it until we all started cryin'. He was a real bastard!" Mr. Teal must have noticed my eyes were wide because he cleared his throat and said, "Sorry, sonny. I forgot you were there. Pardon."

"No problem," I reply.

Papi shoots me a stern look as if to say, "no talking" and I clamp my mouth shut.

"How about one more for the road?" papi asks. Mr. Teal smiles. His teeth are a yellow row of corn kernels. He taps his glass and papi fill it up.

"A toast, to our papas!" papi says rising to his feet, swaying. Some whiskey sloshes over the brim of his shot glass.

"Sorry, I can't drink to that man," Mr. Teal says. "Let's drink to good fortune. I could use some. Ever since the shop fired me, I can't seem to keep a job." He stands up, with a bit of papi's help. They cling glasses.

"To good fortune!" they almost say together.

"May you be a millionaire, someday," adds papi.

Mr. Teal laughs so hard he snorts. Then, he weaves bobbing toward the door. We follow, and I am ready to catch him if he falls. Eyeing the living room couch, he says, "I just need to close my eyes for a minute. He plops down on the blue cushions and kicks off his worn out work boots. His white-gone-to-yellow socks are stinky skunk tails, and I fight the urge to pinch my nose.

"Be a good boy Marco and wake me up in a spell," he says. His eyes flutter and close tight as if sewn shut.

Before I can say "sure thing" he turns on his side facing the back of the couch, almost instantly snoring. Not soft snores either but loud, wall shaking noise.

Papi covers him with a blanket.

All smiles, papi raises a finger to his puckered lips. "Shush. Let him rest."

I nod and papi sways across the room as if onboard a ship and drops anchor onto his recliner. "Turn on the TV, boy."

I turn the TV on. The screen slowly glows until blue light flickers over the red carpet. "What do you wanna watch?" I ask. No answer. White drool hangs on for dear life on the edge of his lips. "Papi?" He is out!

I shrug. Turn the TV off.

My chance to escape, I quietly make my way out the door and roll my old green Huffy Puffy out of the shed down the driveway. I zip through the alleyway, white gravel pinging off the bike spokes.

I stop only to take a look at a dead squirrel. I've never seen a dead one before.

His mouth yawns open, something like papi's and Mr. Teal's snoring. Two big yellow teeth curve down. He could be sleeping, dreaming of prancing across the alleyway with a nut in his jaws. I imagine his frayed tail shaking but it doesn't move. Feeling bad for him, I ride on.

I roll up and down the street where Mr. Teal lives. I picture a man out in his driveway cracking a whip. Imagine he notices me and waves me over, shows me how to crack so it doesn't cut up my face. I imagine cracking the whip once for papa, another time for Mr. Teal, and one giant popping crack just for me.

After a bunch of times of going up and down the street and even around the block several times I lose hope. I feel like crying. My throat closes. My chest is tight. I turn toward home, head down. Then, a few blocks away, almost out of earshot I hear it. The crack! Or is it only just my imagination? Either way, I'll never know. I must go home before papi kills me, and before mama kills papi for letting me run off. Oh los cojones! Damn, I wish I was older, and not some boy on a bike. I would buy a whip. Snap! I would make the air cry! Make el mundo sigh.

Mother and Child by Loomis Mayer
Colored pencil

The Healer by Anne Zimmerman
Needle-felted and fiber art - 9"x15"

Books on my Mind, photo by Jo Liu Press

Immortal kiss in Monet's field, photo by Dia Mariam T

All That Form Allows: The Rothko Chapel
by Selen Ozturk

When I lived in Providence I would wake before the airless damp hour fell, go to the RISD museum at opening-time, sit on a scarred teak bench in a narrow yellow room before a Rothko of blood, cream and persimmon, and remain until closing or until I wept. It was my sole constant; I remember doing nothing else. What is it in us which does not belong entirely to life? Even to ask, one clouds it altogether. I returned to San Francisco before the summer yielded to fall, and nearly before the guard's amusement yielded to disdain. My notes for this piece were, like the testimonies, records, and commentaries I read, only as high as they were vague. However I approached it— biographically, philosophically, empirically—what I saw in Rothko eluded me, only that I could not but look. In Mallarmé's terms I could not convey the thing, but the effect of the thing.

In 1964, Rothko agreed to design the space and supply the paintings for a Catholic chapel under the University of St. Thomas in Houston; he considered it his masterpiece. John and Dominique de Menil commissioned him, demanding no profession of faith. After strife with the Basilians at St. Thomas, they conferred on the Chapel ecumenical (today, interdenominational) status. The spiritual philanthropy of Marie-Alain Couturier, who realized the Matisse Chapel in Vence, informed theirs. To a friend who doubted that Houston would bear such high culture, John replied: "It's in the desert that miracles happen." The chapel was complete in 1971, one year after Rothko's suicide.

The architect—Philip Johnson—yielded to Rothko's demands for the chapel's shape and lighting. Rothko insisted upon an octagonal chapel with an apse, a narthex, two vestries as of early Byzantine churches, and a skylight as in his studio. Paintings were truly seen in the light by which they were painted. By the end of the year he rented a larger studio in Manhattan; by the summer of 1967 Rothko was in Europe with his family and the canvasses were painted. By the next summer he was convalescing in Provincetown in the wake of an aortic aneurysm and a divorce. He over-drank and over-ate. His depression ended with Sinequan and razors.

The chapel holds seven paintings of black over maroon and seven plum tonal paintings, like vacant Stations of the Cross. There are three in a central triptych, six in cruciform side-triptychs, and five lone panels—one facing the apse, and four on facing walls. The largest surpass eleven feet in width and fifteen feet in height. There are plaster-grey walls, flush benches, and a mottled stone floor. Harsh light pours from above. The crimson, flax, and salmon of the forties and fifties yield to hard, dim and retentive hues. A black field lined in charcoal rules half. They are so opaque as to be indistinguishable in pictures. Because he worked with assistants, Rothko's hand has not touched half of these; to whom am I responding? One, Roy Edwards, attested that Rothko could exhaust himself for a month over half an inch. These are resonances of one hard and uneasy idea. They confront their doubles, at once frozen and self-effacing. They deny the hold which his earlier color-fields demand: they are invisible as paintings and tangible as mere objects. The Impressionists knew one century past that darkness admits no resonance; the shifts from blood to coal are delicate and deadpan. Here is less the absence of form than the presence of a mute and solid formlessness.

Regardless, Rothko's break with form was as ambivalent as his early commitment to it: "It was with the utmost reluctance that I found the figure could not serve my purposes... But a time came when none of us could use the figure without mutilating it." He maintained that "there is no such thing as a good painting about nothing... the subject is crucial and only that subject matter is valid which is tragic and timeless." Paintings were truly seen in the feeling by which they were painted. In his own terms, the subject of Rothko's chapel pieces is "basic human emotions—tragedy, ecstasy, doom and so on." With the clear absence of clear figure, one is moved into oneself—tragic, ecstatic, doom-ridden.

But this seems at once too plain and too lengthy. Sadness and happiness are basic emotions; these are neither. After the late forties, Rothko neither explained nor titled his work. When asked to account for these staunch panels, so very near to nothing: "Silence is so accurate." After the opening of his MOMA retrospective in 1961, Rothko came to a friend's door at five in the morning and declared: [I'm] in despair . . . because everyone can see what a fraud I am." The more I look at these, the more difficult it is to imagine a profound reply.

In *Pictures & Tears* (2001), James Elkin posits that "it is likely that the majority of people who have wept over twentieth-century paintings have done so in front of Rothko's paintings." I try to abhor tragedy for tears' sake; there must be some other principle which sets these apart from what Philip Guston called "the sort of paintings people count money in front of." I call a Chapel clerk and ask. She tells me only that they get a lot of cancer patients, people who have taken tests and found that they are dying and people who have taken tests and found that they are not dying. I learn that the base fee for weddings is $2,000; $1,000 for funerals. I tell her that the wake is a bargain; she tells me that it's worth it. Which one, I say.

The tears spent upon our desire bestow no more value upon it. It is difficult to want something which we cannot hold—or which cannot hold us—apart from tears, however provisionally, however delusionally. I believe that Rothko sought not to undo form but to make cohere the eventual formlessness of all forms, not to spurn the seen world but to present its slipping from our grasp. Rothko, again: "It really is a matter of ending this silence and solitude, of breathing and stretching one's arms again." There is an order which only yields and an order which only maims, silence and solitude. I would like to believe that somewhere in the heart there is neither; a silence to live with, a bearable snarl.

Here, vaguely & sheerly: plum into claret, ochre into ash, a clean, bloated, and provisional form to all that light allows. Color confuses itself with its boundary: feathery and raggedly, ink and dusk. Each becomes its opposite until all is melted, scoured, and blurred in a still and pallid swell. It is neither deep nor flat. Here, forms in self-effacing suspension. They are too incongruous and too indistinguishable to tell what is hid and what lost. Rothko wanted them seen in a light low enough to allow "the most subtle vibrations of the color." What tragedies are called through color alone?

Clarity, for Rothko, was a matter of control. To "achieve this clarity is, inevitably, to be understood." His genius renders one's physical relation to the work essential to the work: to look returns one to the event of looking. He was convinced that the paintings would be misunderstood unless he "controlled the situation" in which they were dyed and hung. They stand close and surround serially; here, where he crafts the very space they hold, it has a hermetic quality. The color holds to the line of the canvas, and the paintings to the line of the chapel walls: one form leaves off another, with "no direct association with any particular visible experience... in them one recognizes the principle and passion of organisms." It is an intimacy which smaller works would preclude. If the Chapel had not come Rothko's way, he would have invented it.

Rothko's suicide charged the Chapel's opening with a gloom it would not otherwise have held. The de Menils asked his friend Morton Feldman to compose a tribute; *The Rothko Chapel* was done in months. Rothko once told a reporter that he wanted to convey what Michelangelo conveyed by the Laurentian Library, making one "feel that they are trapped in a room where all the doors and windows are bricked up, so that all they can do is to butt their heads forever against the wall." Feldman maintained that "freedom is best understood by someone like Rothko, who was free to do only one thing—to make a Rothko—and did so over and over again." The space seems both empty and taken, alternately charred and smoldering. Frankly, it rewards no scrutiny. Rothko wanted to paint what "*you don't want to look at.*" Why the same vacancy, over and over again?

Rothko's order in placement and preservation coheres despite, not because of all this repetition: his materials are shoddy and the handling careless. Fifty years later his paintings are dulled, cracked, and roughly dried. During the 1970s they spurred the foulest legal feud in art history: his dealer and accountant seized pieces he willed to his children and to the artists' foundation he intended to establish. I look at them and cannot orient myself but by seeing a tangle of the deep and flat, the near and far. The gulf is part of the unity: the woodwork is eaten by the cost at which its order is wrought. Each becomes its opposite. But there is no tragedy or ecstasy—doom, perhaps—in yielding. The tragedy is that there is no other place, no still point but in the turning. No good painting is about "nothing"; Rothko rather wanted his work to "cover up this 'nothingness'": to veil as it shows, to show without relief.

For one day I did nothing but research this piece. For another, I did nothing but write it. On the third, I sat in the Rothko room at the MOMA. How right, I thought, that before every Rothko there is a

bench. It is said that his genius was for positive and negative space, but here there is neither—only the yielding and not yielding, like some static flood. There is an orange full over oxblood the color of the ground, as the diffused light of a dim day is fuller than the painful light of a bright day. It is unclear where he marks and where he erases. The whole bled into a bar of sapphire, but I could not place where—here the amber gathers the azure, there the olive gathers the ochre. The forms douse each other. It brought to mind the word 'immolation'. I gazed until I felt backed into a corner. To look at a Rothko is an experience I can as little define as master, but suddenly the room *swam* with calm; without grace, without truce. I can only describe it as a dense, blank, deliberately accumulated resonance. It did not yield until the fourth day. Then I felt still.

Rothko patterned the rectilinear planes he painted over and over again from Renaissance tomb compositions. If the Chapel culminates his life's work, it is a raw space out of death: the vault fills to the panel's edge; light rakes from above. Light is all of the world which disturbed Rothko: not merely that *it* changes but that it changes the world between seasons, days, and hours beyond command. The most frequently used word in the guest book by the foyer is "peace": one man affirms that "indeed a sacred feeling filled me and inspired peace and awe", another admits "at a time of turmoil and change a peaceful contemplative respite." There is a place in the heart which does not belong entirely to life. There is no other place. Rothko paints a stillness which moves. "You are in it," he said. "It isn't something you can command." So long as we look, and continue to look, the form slips from our gaze. Perhaps this is all that form allows: space to bear it, for a flash.

Untermeyer Park, photo by Arnold Breisblatt

Goodbye, Brillo; Hello, Fort Apache
by Phyllis Kirigin

There he stood, Mr. Broadbent, the Staff Manager of BBD&O offering me a job as junior executive trainee. **Junior Executive Trainee? With BBD&O**, one of the most prestigious ad agencies in the world? Leading possibly to a career in advertising?

This isn't the way it was supposed to work out. This was just a temp job in the typing pool for the summer to pay my $110 a month rent for my Greenwich Village studio on Charles Street. Oh, did I mention it was 1962?

It was the law. Your first apartment in NYC must be in the Village. I learned that from My Sister Eileen. Even if all you can afford is a studio no bigger than your clothes closet back home and two people can fit in the kitchenette only if they're very emotionally involved, you must live in the Village. And what an exhilarating time to be there. A stroll along Bleeker Street indulged one in the pungent aroma of fresh fish, ripe vegetables, freshly sliced pastrami, heady Gauloise cigarettes, espresso. Woody Allen was testing his comedy chops at The Bitter End, The Sheridan Square Playhouse featured the P. G. Wodehouse musical Leave it to Jane, Paul Newman and Joanne Woodward lived just a couple blocks away on 11th Street and when I so often had dinner at the Lions Head, Ltd. right across the street, the yet to be discovered Jessica Lange waited on me.

I had just finished grad school and was prepared to savor my share of JFK's Camelot. My dream was to be a New York City High School English teacher, to share my love of literature and language and . . . correct punctuation, in September. But it was June and I needed to take the teaching test. I took the train to the dusty NYC Board of Education in Brooklyn, the aroma of which was a prelude to all the musty cloakrooms in my future. The written part went well and then I met the interviewer, a fiftyish woman with her hair in a French roll.

She admonished me, (New York City accent) "Honey, you know you got an accent. 'fathER, mothER, brothER, sistER'? Noooo, It's fatha, motha, brotha, sista. Capeesh? "(pause)

"OK".

She let me slide, accent and all. and I received my assignment—

Samuel Gompers Industrial Arts High School for Boys in the South Bronx. Sounds good. I had a job.

Now all I needed was a temp job. Kelly Girls sent me to BBD&O. Mr. Broadbent, obviously the poster boy for Brooks Brothers, ushered me to the typing pool, a room full of stalwart Remingtons and a small army of living Barbie dolls, each one standing 6 feet tall with her bouffant bee-hive hairdo, stilettos, mini skirt that barely covered her butt cheeks and make-up that had a life of its own.

The typing pool was a whirlwind of tissue paper flying out of shopping bags. Today's shopping finds--The new Wonder Bra, guaranteed to push your boobs up under your chin and create cavernous cleavage. Chit chat reviewing last night's TV shows: Ben Casey, The Dick Van Dyke Show, Perry Mason. And the thickest Queens accents this side of Flushing. "So where do ya wanna eat today, Gladys? The Automat?" And then there was the Schrafft's cart supplying thousands of office workers twice a day with a wonderful caffeine fix.

And through all this I was. . . typing. It's that Puritan work ethic-- growing up believing in "an honest day's work" for . . . Well, you know. BBD&O kept me for the whole summer.

The girls in the typing pool caught wind of my upcoming teaching job. Shirley asked where I was assigned to teach. When I told her it was Samuel Gompers Industrial Arts High School for Boys in the South Bronx, she threw up her arms in shock. It was a battlefield, she told me. There were empty lots full of rubble. It was a bombed-out war zone! There were gangs. They carried guns! I asked her if I could get accidentally shot. She said no, I could get shot on purpose. Maybe I should go back to the Midwest. No. Thomas Wolfe said don't even think about it.

September arrived. I was finishing up my last typing assignment when my boss Mr. Broadbent interrupted explaining that he and the other managers had observed my work and realized that I was clearly overqualified for the typing pool. They had noticed that I could not only type, but spell, fix mistakes and edit. They may have been getting the big bucks, but parallel construction baffled them. This was when he offered me a position as junior executive trainee. Imagine . . . I would be sitting at a real desk in a real office, not just typing copy but creating copy. My imagination went into a frenzy.

Soon I would no longer be a junior executive **trainee**, but a **junior executive**! I would be writing clever prize-winning jingles for Carter's Little Liver Pills, Geritol and the Kodak Pocket Instamatic Camera. I would win a Clio! No more **junior** executive, but **Executive . . . moving . . into . . . the . . . corner . . . office!**

Wait a minute. Was this my dream? My thoughts flashed back to student teaching at Fostoria High School in Ohio showing kids that they could write poetry, that Shakespeare was speaking to them. I remember the heartbreak of seeing the sadness in Lucy Tindall's eyes realizing I would not be back the next year.

And then that corner office reappeared. A **career in advertising**! The ads I could write! I'm young. I think young. I'm in the Pepsi generation! Ring around the collar? I could have written that! A six-figure salary! My tiny studio transformed into a penthouse! Then, the image of Miss Herbst, my high school drama teacher, popped into my head. She had told me that I should go to college. In fact, she took me to visit her alma mater. I stayed over the weekend at a sorority house, went to a Sadie Hawkins Day Dance and saw a production of Macbeth. I knew I had to find a way to get there.

I wanted to have that kind of influence on my students who might need that extra push to realize their potential.

I can't do that selling **Brillo Pads**! Fostoria, Ohio? . . . South Bronx? . . . Kids need a good teacher. I'll take my chances. And, hey, we're in New York City! I can take them to the theater!

Mr. Broadbent raised his eyebrows in anticipation. "Thank you so much for this generous offer, but I can't accept it. You see, I'm going to be a teacher." Mr. Broadbent was dumbfounded. He didn't speak. But I could read his thoughts, "**Allentown**???"

It was quitting time and I placed the cover on my Remington and waved to the Barbies. As I rode down the elevator, the 42 floors of glass wall seemed to dim in the afternoon sun.

Goodbye, Madison Avenue. Hello, South Bronx!

Winter Sun Mask by Claire Duke
Acrylic paint, hot glue, watercolor paper
on paper mâché - 19" x 19" x 6"

My Face has Value by Claire Duke
Acrylic paint and glue
on drawing paper - 10.5" x 9"

Good Advice from a Cup of Joe
by Paul Lewellan

The front door flew open and Constance Pigeon burst into the Cup of Joe clutching The Daily Sentinel. She scanned the café and spotted her target. William Fountain was eating an orange scone and checking the calendar on his iPhone. She slammed the newspaper down on the small table and hissed, "You wrote this crap, didn't you, Bill, you steaming sack of dog shit!"

He noted the headline of the advice column Ask Lannie, "Honest Man Wants Date to 'Woman Up'." The letter writer, who Lannie identified only as Disappointed Male, accused a prospective date of being dishonest and disingenuous. Bill read the opening aloud to his fellow patrons:

> After a fine dinner and entertaining conversation, I told her, "I've had a great time and don't want the evening to end." Because she was always straightforward at work, I was candid. "Let's go to my place for sex."

"Do you have any idea, Constance, how many letters Lannie gets every day?" He looked up. "It's a compliment to be published." Her face flushed. She sputtered, "Every sleaze ball in our building and all the women I work with will know you wrote that about me."

"Now everyone in Cup of Joe knows, too." Bill lifted his coffee cup to salute her. "You must be so proud." Constance wanted to slap him, but he stood up before she could. "I'm getting a refill. Can I get you anything?" He didn't wait for an answer. "Let's talk when I get back."

When Bill returned Constance was seated, but she had not unbuttoned her ski jacket despite the warmth of the coffee house. Bill set three packets of raw sugar and a Café Americano in front of her. Next he set down a plate with two pecan rolls (her favorite) and a second orange scone (for himself). He took his seat and waited, blowing on fresh coffee to cool it.

"What's this?"

"The last time we had coffee here…."

"The only time we had coffee…."

He waved off her qualifier. "You ordered a Café Americano and told the barista to leave room for cream. You picked out a pecan roll and grabbed three packets of sugar that you methodically added during the course of our conversation. I interpreted this as a nervous gesture rather than a sweet tooth, but only you could confirm that interpretation."

The heat of her flushed face faded. He was right. Constance dated her ex-boyfriend Darren for seventeen months, and he never learned her order. Historically, the men in her life didn't listen. Bill reached for his half-eaten scone on the table.

She noted his hesitation. "I didn't poison it, if that's what you're worried about." When that didn't satisfy him, she added, "Didn't spit on it either."

"Good to know." He picked up the pastry and bit. If he wanted to be trusted, he needed to show trust.

Constance popped the lid off her cup, pleasantly surprised that he'd added cream. She poured the first sugar packet into the coffee and began stirring as he finished the first scone. She regretted licking the bottom of it while he was at the counter. That was petty. People sitting nearby saw what she'd done but said nothing. She took a sip of the Café Americano. Perfect. She tried to focus. She hadn't come in to drink coffee. Constance picked up the newspaper and began reading aloud.:

"I'm not the kind of woman who has sex on the first date," she told me. I called her a liar. "If I was Ryan Gosling, or Chris Pratt, or Justin Bieber you'd be that kind of woman."
Why couldn't she be honest? " You're not that hot, and I'm not that desperate. Let's see how the next couple dates go before I commit to sex. Thanks for dinner."

She scowled at Bill. "Justin Bieber? Really?"

"A hypothetical illustration. I'm sure Lannie's readers sensed my point without judging your tastes in men." Several people listening-in nodded in agreement.

Constance suppressed a smile. Bill was a clever man. She'd been working with him for two years at Bailey, Bailey, Manttou, and Deitz. He'd quit a larger law firm in Chicago and moved to Minneapolis after his divorce. Bill had floated in the periphery of her consciousness as she'd dated a series of men she met at her gym, had a brief covert affair with the younger Bailey partner, and been engaged for almost a year by Darren Prough, one of six Commissioners at the Minnesota DNR. That engagement ended abruptly three weeks ago when Constance discovered her fiancé's second cell phone.

"That's not what I meant, Bill."

He glanced at his watch. He was due in court in an hour. He assumed Constance had read the paper on the bus ride in from her new condo in Eden Prairie. She probably hadn't made it to the office yet. Given her agitated state, that was good. "What did you mean?"

She set down the paper and leaned in. "My dating history. I've made mistakes."

"Was dinner with me another mistake?"

"That wasn't what I meant. You're twisting my words." She picked up the advice column. She cleared her throat for everyone listening in to hear this:

Dear Disappointed:
You are most certainly correct. When a date says she's "not that kind of woman," she is being disingenuous, but she is also trying to be nice by not flat out rejecting you. And, yes, she may be waiting for a better offer. James Franco is having a good year. But what did you hope to gain by confronting her?

To avoid future prevarication, perhaps you should be more honest. Tell each potential first date that your preferred dessert is her served on a sexual platter. That gives her the chance to turn you down in advance and save you the price of a meal.
It's a win/win for her, too, because she doesn't waste her time on the likes of you.

Bill applauded. Other people joined in. "That's my favorite part. '...wasting her time on the likes of you.'"

"You think this is funny?" Her anger was back.

"No, I don't."

"What were you thinking when you wrote this?"

"I'll tell you if you take off your coat."

Constance blinked. "I beg your pardon...?"

"You're perspiring. You must be uncomfortable wearing a ski jacket in the heat of this coffee shop. I have a little time before I'm due in court. You're already late to the office, so what are a few more minutes?"

Constance looked at her cellphone and was surprised by the time. She was warm. She took off her coat, poured another sugar packet into her cold coffee, and began stirring. "I'm listening."

"The other night, I thought being 'honest' was clever. But that idea blew up on me. Our first date abruptly ended. I realized there wouldn't be a second. In a petty way I wanted to punish you for that."

"...punish me?"

Bill nodded. "Like you did when you slobbered all over my scone while I was at the counter."

"You saw me?"

"It doesn't matter." He took her hands in his. They were warm. "I wanted things to work out."

"Why?"

"Why not? You've got a fine legal mind, look good in a skirt, and don't put up with my crap. Barging in here with the paper, for example." He stood up and addressed everyone listening in. "What do you think, folks? Do I deserve a second chance?"

"Please, Bill..."

The blonde at the next table piped up. "He thinks he's George Clooney and believes everyone is hot for him." The blonde looked at the other women in the coffee shop for confirmation. "But then all men think that." There was scattered laughter.

The tall skinny barista with the anchor neck tattoo called out. "Lady, he's smart, gainfully employed, and I've heard damned good in bed. If my boyfriend wasn't back from the Marines, I'd be all over him."

A shapely forty-something woman in a tailored suit packed up her briefcase and shook her head in amusement as other ladies weighed in. Constance recognized her from a rival law firm. As the woman passed by on her way out, she leaned down and whispered in her ear, "Honey, when the lights are off, and he's going down on you, you won't care how hairy his eyebrows are."

Constance motioned for everyone to be quiet. "I think Bill and I need a minute."

People returned to their own conversations. The two combatants finished their pastries. When the moment was right, she whispered, "Have you propositioned every woman in here?"

"Thirty percent tops."

"How many had sex with you on the first date?"

"Almost all of them."

Constance blinked again. "But that isn't the critical question."

"What is…?"

"How many did you date a second time?" She took a deep breath. "How many?"

"Only Vivian," he told her, gesturing to suggest the woman who'd just left. "I stopped seeing her when I discovered she was married." Bill squeezed her hand. "You'd be number two."

"I'd have to think about that."

"No problem." He stood up. "Got a court date in a half hour. Let me know at the office." He bent down and kissed her cheek. "But don't dawdle. On Sunday I have tickets on the thirty-yard-line for the Vikings game with the Packers. You could join me." He lowered his voice slightly. "Go Pack."

Constance watched Bill leave the coffee shop. She'd forgotten to thank him for the pastries.

She picked up her coffee cup, but it was empty. She reached for the second pecan roll before she realized she'd already eaten it. She picked up the newspaper, still folded to the advice column, then set it down without rereading it.

"How did he know," she wondered, "I was a Packers fan?"

Finding Polaris
by Laurie Kuntz

You can always pinpoint it
looking for the triangular shine,
I want to learn to find that light
on the nights I'll be alone.
For, so much depends upon
what we leave each other.
Somewhere in the story
is our true north,
directions to travel alone,
to remember to lift our faces,

gaze upward.
We need now to create
new ways to look at old stars.
Even though I would rather dwell
in our past heavens when desire
was in a turn of phrase
and the indigo sky was clearly plentiful.
On those nights, you'd take my hand,
trace beginnings and endings
of constellations that lit our lives.

Golden Sunset, photo by Vinnie Nauheimer

Manon
by August Jane

Beside me Manon's crystal skin is turning cool as her steady breath becomes visible on the pillow. The city pales next to her tragic curls, my eyes following the shine in them as it dances across the wall.

Our open window is bare, allowing the dawn to seep inside. It rises and falls over gorgeous Manon's face, and she breathes it in, exhales the starlight that was gifted to her before I woke.

It is dawn, and I am impatient. There are eggs, still in their shells, still runny, in all that's left of our kitchen. On the counter they sit side by side waiting for the warmth of tea with Manon.

All there is left to do is to wait, and to think. I think of Manon in days past before she loved me, dressed up in satin to gaze at the moon. She never would kiss me then, so I watched as the lovelorn moon looked back into her once-dark eyes. It disappeared so hastily when it saw me at the window with my jealous hands.

Manon's eyes do not belong to me; I have never seen them. To me they have always been pearly, to match the walls. I have made her fit so exquisitely into my world.
Still, though, her eyes are saved only for the moon. These days she only looks when I am sleeping and I awake each morning hungry and alone.
I turn to Manon and shake her gently. I place a sunlit whisper behind her ear and beg her to come back and be everything to me again.

12,766 Fans
by Anita and Myron Pulier

Yo-Yo Ma at Ozawa Hall
Sunday Aug 11, 2019, Tanglewood Mass.
—NY Times

Bach's Six Suites for Cello
clearly not intended
for a massive audience
or an outdoor arena.

The dead are not,
it turns out, inflexible.

Perched on Yo-Yo's shoulder
Johann whispers:
Go for it. Use me.
Untangle these ancient notes.
Strip me bare. Clarify.
Reveal. Teach.

Rapt, we ride the swells,
squirm, blush before the unhurried
exposure of such wrenching intimacy,

thousands of us, gasping,
surprised at the ease with which
one master bears witness
to the immortality of another.

Looking West From My Sister's Property in Emerald
by John Grey

red clay, thin top soil, rocky dunes like ocean waves,
all abandoned here by searing sun's rays,
to be rolled up like a carpet by the night.

So arid, water is the most Christian of the virtues,
tapped from the underground artesian sea,
pumped by pipe and windmill's muscle,
to calm and make something of the rippling sands.

For even in deprivation, there is presence to make known,
surprising resources of determination and survival,
of weather watch and jutted jawline,
that makes my own resilience jealous.

So many reminders here of my inner dust,
the casual breeze swirling the surroundings slow,
making a shadow, not of my body, but of my life,
and a land equal part everything and nothing to do with me.

Electric Pollock by Jennifer Llano
Acrylic on Canvas - 16"x16"

Floating Mariner's School by Michael Mendel
Watercolor - 10"x14"

Orchid on a Snowy Day by Sharon Kullberg
Oil on canvas - 8" x 8"

Rooster Art, by Mike Ryan

Life of Greenhorn
by Zaire Hernandez

Life of Greenhorn
Greenhorn tries to soar
He stumbles, fumbles, and plants
Deep breaths tumble out
Greenhorn awakens
Clouds above slow and scatter
Grasses around coating doubt
Greenhorn approaches
Heart steady yet flight-ready
Wonder racks his mind
Greenhorn disappears
Tomorrow is an oasis
Greenhorn lives once more
He rises, discovers, and stirs
Deep breaths; Move forward
Deep breaths, come out

Human Guidance
by Gary Beck

Imperfect vehicles,
land, sea, air, space,
made by imperfect beings
frequently fail to perform
as optimistically designed,
leaving frustrated operators
stalled, sunk, crashed, marooned
unable at malfunction time
to return for refund,
forced by circumstances
to deal with consequences.

Blue Bird by Red Sagalow
Drypoint Etching and Watercolor - 5" x 6.5"

First Lessons
by Betsy Bolton

Walking backward as instructed, facing
the silken sail, keeping it steady,
I was baffled to hear the instructor

saying my name, telling me not to panic.
I was learning to paraglide: a windy day,
an early lesson, working in a dip

of the hill to stay grounded. Glancing back
at the teacher, I found myself thirty feet above
ground. Rapt. The difference between land and sky

shockingly imperceptible, like a quiet
version of the whirlwind snatching Elijah,
or Paul's third heaven, *whether in the body*

or out of the body I do not know, God knows.
Is that rapture? Miracles made quotidian,
unmiraculous? The week before, I had seen

a man plummet like Icarus to earth, had raced,
panicky, across the pasture toward him
and his triply broken leg, amazed by his stoic

self-possession amid pain and fear. *Don't look
at the brambles*, the teacher said, coaxing me
to turn and face forward, to seek a stairway

back from the clouds. *Body follows vision. Don't look
where you don't want to go.* But I was helpless, rapt,
the thorns snatching me home as I stumbled from the sky.

Interim
by Selden John Cummings

when you hold my face
    each of your hands becomes a continent
        and I become the ocean in between.
I dream of martyrs, and wonder
    while you sleep, why your beauty
        reeks of irritation as if
love made you sensitive
    to the air that ages you
        with weapons too small to see
by the indecent pupil.
    Sometimes I pretend
        that you're growing in my backyard,
thick invisible roots
    caked in dirt like fingers
        flecked with chocolate cake
rooting through my memory
    touch my face again
        and the flask of regret
will have to sell itself
    to the devil.
        When
your hazel irises pebble
    themselves in offshore wind
        that I am come among you,
like an orchid, or an organ player,
    strapping into the emotion
        of the crowd, savoring heart with
the organization of my fingers
    prodding and pulling the chords
        casting forth song after sweet,
sad song into that venomous air
    that wrinkles every sleeping ocean
        flanked by restless continents.

Cordially
by John F. McMullen

I have notes someplace
from the great intellectual
conservative columnist
William F Buckley, Jr

He signed them all
Cordially
I understand that
this was not just for me
he did that with everybody

It was a more polite time
John Kennedy and
Ronald Reagan made
fun of themselves

Kennedy and Goldwater
planned to travel together
to debate – Reagan and Tip
drank together – McCain
defended Obama's patriotism

Is there an inverse relationship
between technological progress
and the decline in cordiality?
Is this what we have wrought?

Do Twitter and Facebook mean
that we will never again have
a Lyndon Johnson and an
Everett Dirkson working
together to reach compromise
for the good of the country?

I wonder if it has
all been worth it

Frameless
by Clarissa Aponte & Roberta H. Dorsett

Our series *Frameless* focuses on experimenting with what photography can be if we negate the camera and the use of traditional photographic film. In our process, we used color motion picture film and black and white darkroom chemicals, and when combined, their reaction resulted in abstract shapes appearing on the film. What developed on the emulsion cannot be found in nature or the world.

Contributors

Gale Acuff (English Dept, Arab American Univ., Palestine) has written three poetry books: *Buffalo Nickel, The Weight of the World,* and *The Story of My Lives*; and published internationally in Ascent, Reed, The Font, Chiron Review, Poem, Adirondack Review, Florida Review, Slant, Arkansas Review, South Dakota Review, and Roanoke Review. asadgale@yahoo.com

Jeffrey Alfier's (Torrance, CA) most recent book, *The Shadow Field*, was published by Louisiana Literature Journal & Press (2020). Journal credits include Copper Nickel, Faultline, Hotel Amerika, New York Quarterly, Penn Review, Southern Poetry Review, and the Vassar Review. Other publications on his website: pw.org/directory/writers/jeffrey_alfier

Karine Leno Ancellin is a professor, writer and translator living in Athens, Greece. She authored a poetry collection -The Missing Angle, published by Riza Press in December 2019. KarineLenoAncellin.net

Cynthia Andersen wrote "*Heart Trouble*" two years ago when she was visiting her mom in FL, who was suffering from heart disease. In addition her mom had broken-up with her boyfriend, and Cynthia wrote the poem. cynanders2000@yahoo.com

Clarissa Aponte (NYC) is a Puerto Rican photographer from Brooklyn and Long Island. She earned her BA in Studio Art and photography from City College of New York, and works as a lab tech in the Visual Media Lab at City College in NYC. clarissaaponte.wixsite.com/photography

Danny Barbare (Greenville, SC) has shown his poetry in over 1,000 online and print journals world wide, won several awards, and has been nominated for Best of the Net by Assisi Online Journal. He studied veterinary medicine at Greenville Tech College. barbaredaniel@yahoo.com

Gary Beck (NYC) is a poet, playwright, novelist, theater director, and art dealer. His poetry, fiction and essays have appeared in hundreds of literary magazines, and his plays have been produced Off Broadway. GaryCBeck.com

Betsy Bolton's (Swarthmore College) work has appeared in Coldnoon and The Poet's Attic. "Worm sex" is forthcoming in The Hopper: Environmental Lit. Poetry. Art. She's served as a Fulbright scholar to both Morocco and Bhutan, where she facilitated the creation of autobiographical videos and filmed miniature documentaries of traditional crafts. ebolton1@swarthmore.edu

Elena Botts (NYC) is a multimedia visual artist and poet. She's published in over a hundred literary magazines, exhibited in local galleries, published numerous poetry books. She graduated from Bard and Johns Hopkins' MA program in international relations. linkedin.com/in/elena-botts-a63202212/

Arnold Breisblatt (Bronxville, NY) is a photographer and Tai Chi instructor. He's on the board of the Westchester Photographic Society, and holds a BFA in Advertising Design and Visual Communications from Pratt Institute. abreisblatt@icloud.com

Tim Brosnan Jr. is a designer in his early 30s whose writing is inspired by his family and friends. He's working on a Master's in English Literature at Mercy College. timbrosnan2@gmail.com

Susana Case was a university professor in NYC. She's written eight poetry books (most recent is *The Damage Done,* Broadstone Books, 2022). She's won a Pinnacle Book Award for Best Poetry Book, and is currently is a co-editor at Slapering Hol Press. SusanaHCase.com

Sabina Colleran (Montrose, NY) holds a BS in psychology from Fordham, and served as content coordinator for Cortlandt Living magazine. She's @wordsbysabina on Instagram and Twitter.

Andrew Courtney (Croton-on-Hudson, NY) is a photographer and documentary film maker focusing on social justice and social responsibility. He's a graduate of Teachers College of Columbia University andrewcourtneyphotography.com

Selden John Cummings (NYC) is a writer and musician living in New York City. His poetry has been published in 86 Logic, Some Kind Of Opening, and Tuck Magazine. He's currently working toward his MFA in poetry at Columbia University. sjc2228@columbia.edu

William Doreski (Peterborough, NH) has taught at several colleges and universities. His most recent book of poetry is *Mist in Their Eyes* (Lulu Press, 2021). His essays, poetry, fiction, and reviews have appeared in various journals. wdoreski@gmail.com

Roberta H. Dorsett (NYC) is an African American photographer from the South Bronx. She earned her BA in studio art and photography from City College in NY, and works as a lab tech in the Visual Media Lab at City College. clarissaaponte.wixsite.com/photography

Mario Duarte (Iowa City, IA) is a Mexican American writer and graduate of the Iowa Writers' Workshop. His poems and short stories have appeared in 2River Review, Abstract Elephant, American Writers Review, Digging Through the Fat, Emerald City, Lunch Ticket, Pank, Plainsongs, Rigorous, Sky Island Journal, Typishly, and Zone 3. Mario-Duarte@uiowa.edu

Claire Duke (Westchester, NY) attends Westchester Community College, and hopes to become an art therapist. CDuke73978@my.sunywcc.edu

Pauli Dutton (La Canada, CA) holds an MLS from USC, and has been published in Verse Virtual, Altadena Poetry Review, Spectrum, and Skylark. Pauli.Dutton@gmail.com

Ellen Elchlepp (Croton-on-Hudson, NY) paints oil portraits on Belgian linen of feminist artists and trail blazers who defied the rules that established society set for them. She holds an MFA from Hunter (NYC) and a BA from UT (Knoxville). She was Senior Art Director at Doubleday Publishing, NYC (1983-2015), and did a cover for *The Soho News*. eelchlepp@optonline.net

R. Gerry Fabian (Doylestown, PA) has published four books of poetry: *Parallels, Coming Out Of The Atlantic, Electronic Forecasts* and *Ball On The Mound*. He's also published four novels: *Getting Lucky (The Story), Memphis Masquerade, Seventh Sense* and *Ghost Girl*. RGerryFabian.wordpress.com

Alan Feldman (Framingham, MA) has a Ph.D. in American Literature, and chaired the English Department at Framingham State. His poems have appeared in *The Atlantic, The New Yorker, The Nation, Poetry, The Kenyon Review, The Yale Review, The Southern Review, Ploughshares, Iowa Review, Threepenny Review, Virginia Quarterly Review*. afeldma@gmail.com

Marcy B. Freedman (Croton-on-Hudson, NY) - has shown artwork in 400+ exhibitions around the country, and has lectured and performed extensively in the tri-state area. She holds an MA from Princeton, an MA from U of Michigan, and a BA from UC Berkley. mbf@bestweb.net

Nora Freeman (Port Chester, NY) - holds an MA in speech and language pathology, and has been working in that field for over 20 years. norafreeman777@gmail.com

Lynne Friedman (Kingston, NY) had solo exhibitions at the James McNeil Whistler Museum (Lowell, MA), The Booth Western Art Museum (Cartersville, GA), and the Woodstock Art Association and Museum

(Woodstock, NY). She's done residencies in France, Ireland, Costa Rica, and Spain. LynneFriedmanArt.com

Diane Funston (Marysville, CA) has published in journals and anthologies including California Quarterly, Cabbages and Kings, GUTS, San Diego Poetry Annual, Snapdragon, Whirlwind, Sharp Piece of Awesome, Lift It Up, Summation, and Palettes and Quills. noparadise@me.com

Fred Gillen Jr (NY) has released eleven full-length albums, and performed all over the U.S. and Europe as a solo artist. His songs have been featured on ABC's "All My Children," NPR's "Car Talk," CMJ's New Music Marathon Sampler. FredGillenJr.com

Jenna Lynn Good (Franklin, TN) born in 2001 in Metro Detroit. She's won two Hopwood awards for poetry at the University of Michigan, where she is majoring in English. jlgood@umich.edu

John Grey is an Australian poet and US resident. He recently published in Sheepshead Review, Stand, Poetry Salzburg Review and Hollins Critic. Latest books, "Leaves On Pages" "Memory Outside The Head" and "Guest Of Myself". Work upcoming in Ellipsis, Blueline, and International Poetry Review. jgrey5790@gmail.com

Kelly Harris (NYC) holds a BA Music fron the University of Chicago and an MA in Musicology from NYU. He's a life-long poet, and you can find him at klh1954@juno.com

Jack Harvey (Delmar, NY) published poetry in Scrivener, The Comstock Review, Valparaiso Poetry Review, Typishly Literary Magazine, The Antioch Review, and The Piedmont Poetry Journal; and been a Pushcart nominee. jharvey@nycap.rr.com

Kathryn P. Haydon (Pound Ridge, NY) has authored four books including her recent poetry collection, *What Do Birds Say to the Moon?* She's the founder of Sparkitivity (sparkitivity.com) kathryn@sparkitivity.com

Zaire Hernandez (Paterson, NJ) is is a Junior (age 16) at John F. Kennedy High School in Paterson, New Jersey. (email care of Thaddeus Cohn, tcohn@ppsstaff.org)

Rachael Ikins (Fingerlakes, NY) has published in India, the UK, Japan, Canada and the USA. She's won several awards for her writing (e.g. 2018 Independent Book Award, 2019 Vinnie Ream & Faulkner). She graduated from Syracuse Univ. RachaelIkins@gmail.com

Stephen M. Jacoby (Croton-on-Hudson, NY) has been writing, drawing, and photographing since childhood. His photos of "Architectural Sculpture in New York City" were published in 1975 (Dover). He's contributed hundreds of art works to collaborative art projects. His photographs and drawings can be seen at Stephen-Jacoby.pixels.com and flickr.com/photos/stephenjacoby/albums.

August Jane (England) is from south-west England, where they are currently studying and doing youth work. Their writing has previously been published in The Star Collective and Tenderness, Lit. augustlshaw@gmail.com

John Kaprielian (Putnam County, NY) is a photographer and photo editor and poet. He's been published in various journals including Poetry Quarterly, Seaborne, and CP Quarterly. facebook.com/366poems

Phillis Kirigin taught high school English in NYC for 34 years before moving to Croton and actively engaging in theater in New York, Vermont, and Nova Scotia. Phyllis died on April 23, 2022. PhyllisKirigin.crotonarts.org

Sharon Kullberg (Croton NY) has been painting for 35 years, and is fascinated by dabs of paint that "magically evoke a panorama or still life glowing with light and depth." She has an MA from Pratt (Brooklyn, NY) and a BA from Northern (DeKalb, IL). sharonkullberg@gmail.com

Laurie Kuntz was nominated for a Pushcart and Best of the Net prize. She has published: *The Moon Over My Mother's House (*Finishing Line Press), *Somewhere in the Telling (*Mellen Press), *Simple Gestures (*Texas Review), and *Women at the Onsen* (Blue Light Press). Her next book is *Talking Me off the Roof (*Kelsay Press, 2022) LaurieKuntz.myportfolio.com

Paul Lewellan (Davenport, IA) has recently published fiction in *Miniskirt Magazine, Jupiter Review, Talon, DASH Literary Journal,* and *CERASUS*. Although he doesn't believe life begins at 70, it does get more interesting after that. plewellan@mac.com

Jennifer Llano (Yonkers, NY) is a self-taught artist, known for her award-winning illustration of Alice & Wonderlands iconic Cheshire Cat at the Syracuse Art's & Craft Festival, and her 24"x 48" acrylic on canvas piece *The Hearts Uncertainty* currently displayed in the *Memento Mori* exhibit at the Riverfront Gallery in Yonkers. jllano1205@icloud.com

Diarmuid Maolala (Dublin, Ireland) published three collections, "*Love is Breaking Plates in the Garden*" (Encircle Press, 2016),"*Sad Havoc Among the Birds*" (Turas Press, 2019) and *"Noble Rot*" (Turns Press, 2022) diarmo90@live.ie

Wendy K. Mages (Greenwich, CT) is a professor at Mercy College, a storyteller, scholar, and an educator. She performs her original stories at storytelling events in the US and abroad, and has published one of her stories in *The Journal of Stories in Science*. WendyMages@gmail.com

Loomis Mayer (Croton-on-Hudson, NY) is retired from a career in publishing, he has attended drawing and painting classes at various times and places over the years and has had exhibits of his portrait drawings and paintings at local libraries and other venues. LMayer@fordham.edu

Anne Maizianne (Westchester, NY) - abstract & figurative artist painter, originally from Belgium. She studied at the Art Students League of New York City, the Art League of Houston TX, and the Glassell School of Art. She's done many exhibitions, commissioned artworks (family portraits), children's book illustration and CD covers. maizianne.art@gmail.com

Janet McCann has published in the Kansas Quarterly, Parnassus, Nimrod, Sou'wester, America, Christian Century, Christianity And Literature, New York Quarterly, and Tendril. She's a 1989 NEA Creative Writing Fellowship winner, and taught at Texas A&M 1969-2016 (now emerita) Most recent is collection is *The Crone At The Casino* (Lamar Press, 2014). mccann1@tamu.edu

Moydan, Michael McKee

John F. McMullen (Yorktown, NY) - is the Poet Laureate of Yorktown, an adjunct professor at Westchester Community College, a graduate of Iona College, the holder of two Masters degrees from Marist College, a member of the American Academy of Poets, and Poets & Writers, and author of over 2,500 columns and 12 books (10 poetry). johnmac13.com

Michael Mendel (NYC) designed record album covers for over 35 years for some of America's great recording stars. (Tony Bennett; Donovan; Beach Boys; The Hollies; Stylistics) and also designed album covers for Original Broadway Show Recordings and Motion Picture Soundtracks (Godfather; Serpico). mbgreateam@gmail.com

Robert Milby (Florida, NY) is a freelance writer, who has been reading his poetry in the Hudson Valley, NYC, Long Island, NJ, PA, and New England since 1995. He's given over 450 featured readings, and self-published four books. RobertMilbyPoetry.com

Vinnie Nauheimer (Croton-on-Hudson, NY) has photographed Hudson River Sunsets for the last twenty years. When he's not taking pictures, he also paints and writes. facebook.com/davincechi

Susan Obrant (Cortlandt Manor, NY) has done Grammy-nominated album covers, an exhibition at MOCA Peekskill (2016-2018), and West Conn Univ (2025). Her couture crochet has costumed the Heidi Latsky Dance Company, the actress Audra McDonald, and Violinist Daisy Jopling at Lincoln Center. SusanObrant.com

Selen Ozturk (San Francisco) was born in Istanbul and raised in the Bay Area. She studied painting at RISD and philosophy at UC Berkeley. Recent publications include Monday Journal, Spring Journal, Bright Lights Film Journal, and the Penn Review of Philosophy. selen@berkley.edu

Jess L Parker (Madison, WI) poetry collection, *Star Things,* is winner of the 2020 Dynamo Verlag Book Prize. Her work has appeared in *Ariel, Poetry Hall, Millwork, Kosmos, Bramble* and elsewhere. She holds an MA in Spanish Lit from UW, Madison and an MBA JessLParker.com

Kevin Pilkington (Westchester, NY) is on the writing faculty at Sarah Lawrence College. He's written two novels and ten collections of poetry, most recently *Playing Poker With Tennessee Williams* (Black Lawrence Press). His new novel *Taking On Secrets* will appear later this year by Blue Jade Press. kpilking@slc.edu

Jo Liu Press (Cortlandt Manor, NY) paints and photographs, and is self taught, You can find her at sombreuill@aol.com

Anita Pulier (NYC and LA) is a poet (and retired lawyer), and her husband Myron is an illustrator (and psychiatrist). Her poems have appeared in nine anthologies, and several online and print venues: *The Writer's Almanac, The Linnet's Wings, Your Daily Poem, The Los Angeles Times, etc.* psymeet.com/anitaspulier/

Fred Pollack (Washington, DC) published *The Adventure* (Red Hen Press) and *Happiness (*Story Line Press), *A Poverty Of Words* (Prolific Press) and *Landscape With Mutant* (Smokestack Books, UK). He's appeared in Salmagundi, Poetry Salzburg Review, The Fish Anthology (Ireland), Magma (UK), Bateau, Fulcrum, Chiron Review, and Chicago Quarterly Review. fpollack@comcast.net

Jack Powers (Fairfield, CT) is the author of *Everybody's Vaguely Familiar*. His poems have appeared in The Southern Review, The Cortland Review and elsewhere. He won the 2015 and 2012 Connecticut River Review Poetry Contests and was a finalist for the 2013 and 2014 Rattle Poetry Prizes. JackPowers13.com/poetry/

Ken Pobo (Media, PA) most recent books are *"Lavender Fire, Lavender Rose"* (BrickHouse Books) and *"Sore Points"* (Finishing Line Press). He's retired from teaching at Widener University, and lives with his husband and two cats. Twitter: @KenPobo

George Robinson is a teacher and nature photographer. His latest book series is *The Central Park Statues Speak.* He writes a newsletter *On the Road to History,* and teaches writing at Western Connecticut State University where he's the Associate Dean of Evaluation and Accreditation for Bridges Graduate School of Cognitive Diversity in Education. Geo.Robinson@hotmail.com

Mike Ryan (Peekskill, NY) is a visual artist and teacher. He holds an MFA in Graphic Design from Savannah College of Art & Design, a BFA in Computer Arts & Design from Mercy College. He's taught at Mercy College, The College of Westchester, Savannah College of Art & Design (TA), and Westchester Community College. Mike-Ryan-Art.com

Red Sagalow (NYC) holds an MFA in Studio Arts from City College NY., and was awarded the Therese McCabe Rolston Connor and Social Impact awards. He's shown in Los Angeles, Phoenix, and New York; and published in the Harpy Hybrid Review in 2021. RedSagalow.com

Vera Kewes Salter (New Rochelle, NY) was born in England to a family of refugees from Nazi Europe. She holds a Ph.D in Sociology. She writes at the Hudson Valley Writers' Center. Her most recent publications are in *Nixes Mates Review, Prometheus Dreaming, Right Hand Pointing, Judaica, Medical Literary Messenger*. verasalter@gmail.com

Laurie Steinhorst (NY) has an MFA from Hunter College, NY and BFA from MA College of Art, Boston, MA. She teaches in the Computer Arts Department at Mercy College, White Plains, NY; and has had several exhibitions. LaurieSteinhorst.com

Dia Mariam T (Ballyvaughn, Ireland) is a photographer, writer, and illustrator; working on her masters in Studio Arts at Burren College of Art. She grew up in India, and most of her art involves commentary on social issues and taboos. diyamariam4@gmail.com

Tom Tarnowski (Croton-on-Hudson, NY) has a BA in English. He works with a non-profit group, Friends of the Old Croton Aqueduct, that manages (in partnership with NY State) the 26 mile long old aqueduct trail in Westchester. Tom.Tarnowski@gmail.com

Lynda Coupe Wolfe (Mohegan Lake, NY) has a Ph.D in English and is a retired high school teacher and college professor. She's published *Images of the Hunter in American Life and Literature* (Peter Lang Publishing, 2000), and presented papers and chaired sessions at many conferences. cwl12903@aol.com

Christopher Woods (Chappell Hill, TX) is a writer and photographer. His novella, *Hearts In The Dark*, was recently published by Running Wild Press. His poetry chapbook, *What Comes, What Goes*, was published by Kelsay Books. instagram.com/dreamwood77019/

Pam Zicca (Peekskill, NY) is a photographer and swimming instructor. Her latest book of photography, *Nature as a Sanctuary: Seeking Refuge in the Pandemic*, was self-published on Amazon in 2021. PamZicca.crotonarts.org

Anne Zimmerman (Ossining, NY) is an artist, art teacher and certified therapeutic art life coach. She studied at the College of New Rochelle. facebook.com/search/top?q=anne zimmerman

Made in the USA
Middletown, DE
25 June 2022